I0737669

Ursula's Inheritance

American Civil War Brides Book 3

By Eileen Charbonneau

Print ISBNs
Amazon Print 978-0-2286-1986-4
LSI Print 978-0-2286-1987-1
B&N Print 978-0-2286-1985-7

http://bwlpublishing.ca

Dedication

For my fellow Scribe Sisters, Juilene Osborne-McKnight, Eileen O'Finlan, and Jane Willan who helped immeasurably to get me into the writing harness for this one.

And with deep thanks to all the readers of Mercies of the Fallen who said, "What happens next?"

Chapter One ~ Rowan

April 1864, Gramercy Park, Manhattan

Even with the one eye the war had left him, Rowan Buckley knew the wee one pilfering from the garden was a girl, despite her trousers. He frowned at the canvas bag at her feet.

"So it is not a squirrel with an interest in our angelica, then?" he asked quietly.

The urchin turned, startled eyes narrowing. "Better me than an Irish thug!" She spat.

The girl took advantage of his hesitation and his limited depth perception. She grabbed the sack and raced toward the iron garden gate. But after three hard years of soldiering, there was nothing wrong with Rowan's reflexes. He caught up, took her wrist, and, when she resisted, her waist. She had a waist. So she was a little older than her small size had first impressed upon him.

"Please let me go, sir," an even smaller voice came out of her.

"Am I 'sir' then, now that you're caught?"

"You are a black Irish scoundrel to hold me against my will!"

She kicked him. Hard enough to throw off his stance. He maintained his temper and light grip as he steered her toward the tradesman's door of Ursula's house.

"You've nothing to fear from me, lass." He sent her through the entrance with a nudge at her back. "Now hush up your caterwauling, the baby's asleep."

Jonathan was stretched out at the hearth, his stockinged foot rocking the cradle. His eyebrow arched.

"Company? The kettle's on, my fine fellow."

"Your fellow is a girl, and there's nothing fine about her," Rowan corrected, lifting the cap off his captive's head. Fair-haired braids descended. "May I present our angelica and camomile thief?"

Jonathan smiled. "Ah. Mystery solved."

The girl's eyes fired. "I planted that garden!"

"Did you?" Jonathan asked in his most charming southern tone. "Fetch the young horticulturist a chair, brother."

"She kicks," Rowan warned.

The girl's light brown eyes narrowed as she looked from one to the other. "You're not brothers."

"And you neglected to pay for your trousers," Rowan observed, yanking off and reading the dry goods store tag. "The proprietor might want a word with you about that."

"The proprietor is my father. His name is Selby, see?"

A rustling of nightclothes and Ursula stood in the back doorway. "Mr. Thomas Selby?"

Rowan saw something familiar in the girl's trapped look, the tears stubbornly held back.

"You are so confusing! All of you!" She shouted loud enough to startle wee Henry to wailing.

"Aw, there now then, fledgling," Rowan soothed, lifting the baby from the cradle and into his arms. "You've had enough of the lot of us, have you?"

Ursula kept her eyes fixed on the girl.

"What is your name?"

"Penina."

She glanced in the sack, "Thank you, Penina. A little camomile is exactly what we need for our Henry's teething gums. Take the rest home. Will you not join us for breakfast first?"

Rowan sighed. His wife had found another stray. He rubbed his sore shin, then fetched the frying pan. This little one might enjoy some of his oatcakes, he supposed.

Chapter Two ~ Penina

Penina sat quietly in the kitchen of what used to be her own home. Everything was different, save this rough-hewn worktable and the old, sturdy yoke back chairs. The hearth hung with bunches of familiar herbs, but the brick walls were now whitewashed, and her mother's corner cupboard displayed teapots and crockery ware of a fine quality. There was a new dry sink, and a cookstove that was a gleaming replacement of the cranky Franklin stove. Penina had thought of the widow as her enemy, wicked and old, like stepmothers in fairy tales. Not this quiet, beautiful woman putting a robust baby to her breast as two young, beardless men bustled about the kitchen looking after her and serving breakfast, the most delicious breakfast Penina had ever eaten.

"Why does this taste sweet?" she asked.

"That would be from his relatives," the light-haired man said, wiggling his thumb at the other, the dark, bigger Irish one working at the stove. "He douses bacon in maple syrup. Now, I prefer honey cured myself. Back in Maryland, we had—"

Penina dropped her fork. "This is bacon?"

"Yes. In that peculiar Canadian cut of it," he told her, taking up the carving knife. "Would you care for some more?"

"No!"

All of them stopped moving. Even the baby lifted his head from his mother's breast and stared at her. Penina felt her throat constrict. Tears threatened. Not their fault, she heard her father's voice. Do not blame the Christians. Yes, Papa. She should have asked. She should have asked.

"A fresh plate for Miss Selby's new oat cakes, if you would, Rowan dear," the widow said quietly before lifting the left part of her bodice transferring the rooting baby to that side.

"Of course, my love."

The steaming cakes went from his spatula to a spotless piece of blue and white import china ware, before switching it for her own, the one with only morsels of its pork remaining.

The smaller, light-haired man put down his knife and quietly poured tea for her and the widow, fresh coffee for himself and the cook. Penina noticed the men's trousers now, blue wool with a red stripe down the side. They were soldiers.

The cook threw a towel over his broad shoulder and thumped a heavy glass pitcher with amber liquid before her. "Try more maple syrup, lass."

She ventured a look at him. "Thank you, sir. But I am not hungry."

"No wonder," the light-haired man observed. "You ate enough for—"

"Jonathan," the widow silenced him with a gentle, scolding look before she turned back to Penina. "You miss the garden?" she asked.

"My father said we must be grateful, because our house is now large and comfortable, and so close to the shop."

"That is what my property agent Mr. Gardner assured me last year, that the tenants were happy with our arrangement. But he never asked you or your mother, did he?"

"Papa speaks for the family."

She was in trouble now. For letting out a resentful tone.

But the widow only said, "I see," in that soft way, before looking up at her companions. "Miss Selby and her parents rented this house before me, my darlings," she told them. "This was her home."

The light-haired man frowned, but his companion put another heavenly smelling pancake on her plate. "Try one with the peach butter, lass," he urged, "if you don't fancy the maple."

"You and your peaches," the other groused. They did act like Penina had seen brothers act toward each other.

The baby released, sat up, then patted his mother's breast and belched.

They all laughed. The man who had captured her in the garden appeared most pleased. "Well, eaglet," he said, caressing the baby's head, "You have enjoyed your breakfast!"

Another frown from the light-haired man. "He has his father's manners."

The widow's eyes darted between the two before she held the baby out to the dark one.

Who was this woman? And these men, her "darling" soldiers, cooking for her, eating with her in their open vests and rolled up shirtsleeves? There were rumors. Of Mrs. Major flouting every decency as she consorted with actors and artists. And now soldiers. How did a war widow live as comfortably as she did, people asked, with both negro and Irish servants waiting on her?

So far, no servants had appeared in the kitchen, only these two men, laughing and teasing each other, doting on the widow and her baby. Say something, Penina admonished herself. Years of working with her parents in the shop had made it easy for her to talk to strangers.

But not these strangers. "Our new place has no room for a garden," she finally offered. "We tried to grow herbals at the windowsill, for my father's health, but they did not take."

"Well," the widow said, putting a graceful finger to her cheek. "We will have another key made for the garden gate."

"What?" the flaxen-haired man objected.

But she silenced him with that fierce look before her voice turned sweet again. "You may come whenever you like, Penina. Keep us company. Help me plant and harvest, if you'd like. And take whatever you need home. Your father is ailing?"

"Since the riots. He had the store barricaded, we were all inside, quiet and safe, but he left us to help our last customer, a negro sailor man. The mob and their pikes and guns came inside, screaming at the man. They wanted to hang him, burn him. Papa sent him out the back way, and down an alley. So those

Irish," she cast a glance around, "they beat my father instead. And wrecked and burned our store."

"Dia ár sábháil!" came from the man at the stove.

"Do not you curse us!"

The slender man rose. "He is not cursing you, Miss Selby. Rowan," he commanded. "Translate."

"God save us," the big man said softly. "It was a prayer, Miss."

Penina stared at her hands, tried to blink the tears from her eyes.

The woman's long, beautiful fingers covered hers. "Perhaps you men might take our Henry for a walk in the morning air, and leave us ladies be for a few moments?"

They reached for their coats like obedient children, swaddled the contented baby, and were out the tradesman's door before Penina knew what was happening.

"Penina. I am so sorry to have caused you pain, however inadvertently."

"You have not done that, Ma'am."

"Inconvenience, then. Are there friends here in Gramercy Park of your acquaintance?"

"No, Ma'am, no friends. We worked long hours at the shop."

"We? Tell me about your life, Penina. Do you attend school?"

"I have completed my schooling, Mrs. Major."

"Surely not, child."

"I am not a child! I am fourteen!"

"Oh, I beg your pardon."

"I am small for my age, always taken for years younger. It is not your fault." Why was she excusing the woman? Because she looked so mightily sorry, instead of the insults that usually came with discovery. 'Fourteen is it? You must eat more, girl!' or 'Don't your parents feed you?'

The widow smiled. "Your disguise was most clever for keeping yourself safer on these city streets before daybreak. But I hope you will allow my Rowan or Jonathan to accompany you on your return home."

"Who are those men?"

"Oh, I beg your pardon again, for their rudeness in not introducing themselves. They are used to camp life, across the river on Rikers Island. Sometimes I fear they forget their manners. They are my dearest friends, Captain Rowan Buckley and Sergeant Jonathan Kingsley. My family. And they would not hurt you for the world, Penina."

Penina tried to remember the widow's words as she walked beside Sergeant Kingsley, now in his full military gear, up Broadway. One gloved hand balanced the carefully packed container of spring herbal seedlings, but he rested the other on his sword's hilt, as if wondering if she would snatch it out of its fancy scabbard. Still, he did not hurry her along, as many longer-limbed people did, but matched his pace to hers. And she was dragging her feet, hoping her mother had not checked her bedroom yet and discovered her gone again.

Caroline Selby stood in their doorway, scanning the street, looking careworn and worried. Penina should not have stayed for breakfast, even if it meant she now had a full box of Captain Buckley's oatcakes under her arm. And how was she going to explain the trousers she wore, snatched from the boxes of ready-made clothes salvaged after the fire?

"Mother, may I present Sergeant Kingsley, who—"

"Hopes these plants might prove useful, Ma'am," he finished, stepping forward. "I bear a note of introduction from my— from Mrs. Major, who welcomes your family to the bounty of Gramercy Parks's herb garden, which we understand was begun by way of your own efforts."

Caroline Selby took the note, but her eyes stayed on Sergeant Kingsley. "Penina. You have gone back there again."

"Yes, Mama."

Her mother's grip crushed Mrs. Major's note. "Please dress. The hospital has sent for us. Papa …has taken a turn."

"A turn? Mama, what does that mean? He was doing so well. They said he could come home!"

"Might I accompany you, Ma'am?" Penina heard the sergeant ask as she slipped past them, dread circling her heart.

Chapter Three ~ Jonathan

Jonathan Kingsley was used to hospitals, and this was a finely appointed one, with clean linens and many of what his sister had once been, dedicated nursing nuns, floating from bed to bed, easing men out of their suffering or their lives. He did not want to be here. These were not soldiers, but civilians, victims of the summer's Draft Riots, a week of barbarity unlike anything Jonathan had ever seen, even in battle. Without his more war-hardened brother-in-law commanding him, without his sister and little Henry to look after over the birth and confinement, he wondered if he could have made it through those days fueled by hatred and fear. This hospital still housed the aftermath, as sure as those bloodied floors under the doctors' feet after Gettysburg. They were twin horrors that haunted his dreams.

He and Rowan had helped bring down the burning rope still blowing on the summer wind from lamp-posts where men had swung. They had served guard duty among the burnt-out buildings, the broken storefronts in the first months after the riots. Did the mob find the sailor who Penina's father had sent down the alleyway? Or had he and Rowan buried the man's charred remains? Too late. Why were they too late to save more lives?

He did not have to be here in this hospital, now, amidst this continued suffering. Still, there was something in Mrs. Selby's desperate, lost expression that prompted the offer to abide with the little thief's family a while longer. Or maybe it was the little thief herself, bravely bearing a burden she should not have.

Thomas Selby's nose had been broken, most likely, from the sound of his labored breathing. It had not healed correctly from the time of the riots, Jonathan suspected. And what other injuries afflicted the thin body under the neatly tucked covers of his bed? Somehow the man's deep-set eyes were familiar. His daughter was familiar too, especially now that she was out of her trousers and in a green dress, her wild golden curls bouncing. She had turned from truculent child into the most charming of misses.

"This is our new friend, Papa," she called her father out of his half sleep. "And he has brought you the most delicious oat cakes this morning!"

"Ah, my beauties have found themselves a handsome champion of the first order—a red sash officer!"

"I am only a sergeant, sir. The sash is ceremonial."

The man's laugh had a rattle that Jonathan had heard too many times before. Still, those merry eyes continued defying the inevitable as he pulled in air to speak.

"My best friend on the ward, is a sergeant too, of our metropolitan police force. He came from guarding orphans to assisting my brave women in hauling my helpless hulk on an ambulance wagon. His reward? Being beset by the mob as well. And so, we both ended up here. You must meet him. We have been looking after each other these past months. And our families visit us every day! Are we not fortunate, sir?"

"Indeed."

"He will appreciate your cakes more than I, for after last night's overindulgence, I have lost all taste except for my beautiful women. Sergeant Harrigan! Are you there, sir?"

The bed beside his was empty.

"We will make sure that Sergeant Harrigan is fed, dear," his wife whispered.

He reached for her hand, held it. "Now then, Caroline. You must evict that scoundrel boarder in his brocade waistcoats and rent the spare rooms to our sergeant."

"What a splendid idea, Papa!" his daughter chimed in. "Sergeant Harrigan sings all the latest minstrel songs so well!"

The laugh caught in her father's throat this time. Jonathan didn't like the sound of the hoarse coughing that followed. Not at all. The girl's eyes met his. They filled with fear and panic. Like his own, he suspected, in the midst of battle. He sat on the bed and held the merchant's thin form higher in his arms until he quieted. Damnation. Why hadn't Rowan come too? He was better at this. Jonathan wanted the sound of their little eight-month fledgling's well-fed chortle, not this. No more of this.

The man's voice faded to a raspy whisper, as his shaking finger approached, touched Jonathan's face.

"Young Master Jon?" he whispered. "Is it you, that child pining for your sister? Are you now grown into your manhood?"

"Sir?"

"Listen. I did what you asked of me. I delivered her comb."

"Comb?"

Jonathan looked into the sunken black eyes, around the hairline now white where it once was sprinkled with grey, to the ear, and there, yes, behind it, the mole, shaped like a turtle. He remembered it. He remembered him.

"Mr. Shulmann?"

"Your sister. I delivered her comb. And she gave me a pearl in return. You must thank her, please." The grip on the sergeant stripes of Jonathan's coat sleeve tightened. "Will you thank her, Young Master Jon?"

"Yes. Yes, of course, Mr. Shulmann."

"Ah, then, perfect. What a wonderful day!" His head fell back against Jonathan's chest.

His wife sobbed quietly. But his daughter screamed out her grief.

Chapter Four ~ Ursula

There were few occasions when her brother was at a loss for words. Ursula took his hand, held it there at his knee. A spring breeze wafted past the lace of her drawing room's windows. He pulled it in with a shuttering breath, like when he'd be trying to show her how brave he was when his hand was caught in a slammed door as a child. She felt so rich in feeling men, between her husband, brother, and their little nursling.

"Oh, Jonathan. How terribly sad."

"Ursula," he warned. "Do not cry." He handed her a linen handkerchief from his waistcoat pocket.

But it was too late. Her own breaths were coming in great heaves. "I'm afraid I cannot help it. Our Miriam says to tell you, if you get cross with me, that I cannot help it. Marie Agathe agrees."

He laughed. "Is there nothing upon which those two guardians of your motherhood disagree? And does Baby HRB not do enough crying for both of you?"

"Why, Jonathan," she huffed at him, "you know Henry is a jolly fellow. He only cries when necessary."

"And the same is true for you?"

"I suppose. Only it is more necessary these days, the ladies say."

He swiped his nose with the back of his hand, causing her to frown at him as if he were still seven. "Well. Perhaps Miriam can conjure up a good excuse for me."

"Perhaps." She leaned over to kiss his forehead. "If you stay on her good side."

Miriam had encircled them both in her no-nonsense embrace after their mother's disastrous second marriage. Ursula often wondered at the miracle of an enslaved woman enlarging her heart to care for two lonely children of her mistress, even after Magnus Kingsley had treated her own three— Sling and her twin girls Dibb and Nima, with such contempt. And when Ursula returned from the convent as the new mistress of Fenwick Pines, Miriam became something more: her friend. One who escaped with her into the North after the spy catchers threatened them both. Miriam was now leading her own life in Brooklyn, thanks to Marie Agathe taking over her duties. Ursula missed her friend being in charge of her Gramercy Park household, but both women, the tall French Canadian one, and the diminutive but powerful one born into slavery, now doted on her and the baby. And Miriam was more safe in Brooklyn after Manhattan's draft riot horrors. Ursula would do anything to keep her friend and what was left of her family safe.

"Ursula, listen to me," her brother called her out of her thoughts and back into their childhoods. "Right before you went away to the convent. Do you remember I made you a comb?"

"Of course. Out of the ash limb that was struck by lightning. Full of the hoo-doo, Miriam said, remember? I use it every day even now, dear heart. It has only grown stronger, more seasoned over the years."

"But you did not take it with you, back then, when you left us!"

Jonathan's voice was suddenly filled with the hurt of the abandoned child he had been. This was important, Ursula realized. Because it was painful to return to those days, for both of them. He had always disguised his pain before, with humor, or flashing anger. This was different. His hurt was undisguised, and true.

"You are right," she said carefully. "But Sister Raphaela delivered it to me soon after I arrived at the convent. And so, I have it still."

"Who brought it to her?"

"My. I never asked," she realized now.

"Mr. Shulmann."

"Mr. Shulmann? The peddler?"

"Yes. He tromped all over Maryland with his cart, remember?"

Ursula nodded. "Of course. Such a kind man. And so patient with us and our questions…starting with why his first name was a name our neighbors gave to their slaves."

"Aaron! Yes, I remember."

"'Because they think God of my people, in the Hebrew part of their bible? They believe blesses what they do, young ones,' he told us, 'to other children of God.' Do you remember that, brother?"

Jonathan turned into her secret confidant again. "Yes. He always told us those things quietly. He trusted us, did he not? And I remember those stories of his travels to find his treasures in New York, and his beautiful wife waiting for his return every Sunday to the city of Baltimore. We were always happy to see his cart. He was our Turtle Man."

Ursula laughed. "Yes, you called him that, when you were little. Because of a mole."

"He trusted us, so he was the only one I trusted."

"Trusted?"

"With your comb! Kindly stop repeating the last word of my every sentence, sister. When you went away, no one told me where, or why. I begged him to find you, to give you the comb. So you would not forget me."

"Oh, Jon."

"I never saw him again. But he must have found you, before he disappeared."

"Disappeared?"

"You are doing it again."

"I beg your pardon. I am trying to understand."

He drew in a deep breath. "No, forgive me. Sometimes I forget how tightly they sealed you away. Ursula, Mr. Shulmann stopped coming to Fenwick Pines. Disappeared from the Eastern Shore all together. Now I know where he went. To the New York of his stories. Not just to fetch his boxes of needles, pins, silk handkerchiefs and pocketknives. To set up a shop, with his wife and daughter. He is the man who died this morning."

"But, Jonathan, Penina's father is Mr. Thomas Selby."

"Have you ever met your tenant, this man Selby?"

"Well, no. But that is not unusual. Mr. Gardner is my go-between with tenants."

"Yes, Mr. Gardner, your counselor, who manages your investments and properties, and who is yet to trust that Rowan and I have no interest in your inheritance. I shall leave his interrogation to you. Me, I will deal with the Shulmanns. I have yet to discuss our connection with his widow in her new bereavement. But I am convinced that Thomas Selby is our Mr. Shulmann. Right to that turtle mole behind his ear."

"Many people have moles."

"But not many of them want to talk about combs with their last breaths."

"Jonathan. What did he say?"

"I am to thank you. For the exchange of your pearl for the comb delivery."

"Pearl? But I never gave him anything."

"That is not what he said. On his deathbed, sister."

"Oh, Jonathan." Ursula saw her mother's necklace ripped from her neck, its pearls scattering among the glass shards of broken wine bottles on the root cellar floor, before his hands crushed around her neck, choking the life from her in his rage. Muting the screams. Screams that still lived inside her. She had salvaged none of those pearls to give Aaron Shulmann for the comforting gift of her brother's comb. Say something. You are frightening your dear brother, who has already had a trying day.

"What could he have meant?" she finally pushed out.

His familiar crooked half smile was her reward. "Men see all sorts of things when they are dying, remember? The ones after the battle at Antietam took you for their mothers and sisters and wives as you held their hands and sang them out, remember?"

"That is true. But Mr. Shulmann knew you, Jonathan. He knew you before you knew him. And you were a little boy when he saw you last."

"Yes. I did seem to make a lasting impression."

"This is important!"

He drew closer and held her hands between his. "Listen. I do not like the look of you. We will find out how all this fits. Together. Do not let it worry you, sister."

"We have already impeded our own efforts."

"How?"

"Aaron Shulmann was of the Hebrew faith. I suspect that did not change with his name. And we fed his daughter bacon this morning. Remember her sudden loss of appetite?"

Jonathan let out a blast of laughter. "An honest mistake!"

"I must ask her forgiveness and speak with her mother. Oh, to have added to their sorrows at a time like this. And Jonathan, how is it that Mr. Gardner rented this house to our dear peddler man, a man from our lives at Fenwick Pines?"

"An interesting question."

Ursula had the strangest sensation that her world was turning upside down. Was that an effect of being a new mother, too? She must ask Miriam. And she must make an appointment with her solicitor.

Mr. Gardner bustled around his office, pulling folders off shelves, rifling through them. Both his balance and speed belied the man's advanced years.

Ursula had inherited Mr. Gardner from her father. He was the family's trusted agent since an unexpected inheritance turned Baby Henry's namesake from a pampered third son of an English earl to a man of wealth and property, most of it connected to the slave trade. He had Mr. Gardner to help him replace all those linked investments and put the proceeds into this city that he loved. Her father's letters to her mother throughout those 1840s described Mr. Gardner as an old man, even then.

He opened another drawer, muttering. Was his age finally causing some mental infirmity, Ursula wondered. Perhaps one of his clerks in the outer office could assist him?

Ursula brought Henry to the street side bay windows of Mr. Gardner's sanctum. Together they looked out at the wide expansive view of the jumble of buildings and church spires. Every time she came here, it seemed the view had changed. New York was a city in constant transformation. The baby delighted in the draft horse pulling a wagon full of hemlock-tanned leather hides below, destined to make shoes for marching soldiers, perhaps. Another reminder of the war he'd been born into. Then her darling boy found nearer interest in the silk tassels on the lawyer's red and gold brocade drapes.

"The Selby lease is here somewhere..." Mr. Gardner found a paper and stared at it. Surely leases were not written on half sheets?

As much as his unkempt iron-grey beard gave him the look of a grizzled John the Baptist, Ursula had never known her solicitor to be anything but organized and efficient during her visits. This haphazard bumbling had nothing to do with his advanced years, she surmised now. It had a purpose that gave Ursula an unsettled feeling, again, of her world going askew. Or was it her hat? Yes, Henry had knocked it sideways. She and Marie Agathe laughed at his antics.

"Perhaps his maman will allow petit caneton to visit with the driver below," Marie Agathe suggested. "For regardez, he stops to feed his horse, I think."

Ursula smiled. "A grand idea, Tante."

Marie Agathe held up the sock doll infused with chamomile. "Avant, mon rayon de soleil?" she coaxed.

Henry clapped, went easily into her arms and they headed for the door.

Ursula inhaled the remnants of her child's scent as it was replaced by Mr. Gardner's ink and ledgers. She approached his desk.

His light eyes shone above the rims of his spectacles. But his mouth formed into a frown. "How well do you know this woman, my dear?"

"Miss Belanger is one of the three French Canadian sisters who raised my husband after he lost his family to Ireland's Great Hunger, sir. He calls them his 'three Maries.'and so Marie Agathe Belanger is Henry's beloved aunt. She has been with us since Miriam joined her family on their farm in Brooklyn after Christmas."

"Her command of English— "

"Is not as proficient as that of the sister who manages Fenwick Pines, Marie Madeline, yes."

"But I thought that woman's name is Picard."

"Madame Picard, yes. She is the eldest and a thrice-married widow."

"The woman sounds dangerous."

Ursula laughed. "'Formidable,' I believe is the word my husband uses. And she is worldly and full of life, as her younger sister is home-loving, but she not at all dangerous, if you do not cross her, sir. And Fenwick Pines thrives in Marie Madeline's good hands, as you have observed yourself in her detailed reports. The sisters' Quebec farm is now run by Marie Catherine. Rowan says she is a fine cook, and with that skill retains the best field workers at planting and harvest times. He is teasing, of course, but I suspect there is some truth in it. The sisters must miss each other. Marie Agathe has had the least contact with the world outside their farm, but Rowan remembers her as most tender with him when he was very young. The sisters agreed on the choice, and so it was decided. Think on this, sir. Marie Agathe has traveled all the way to this loud, boisterous city to help us. Is she not the bravest of women? Henry will soon babble in both French and English! Is that not wonderful?"

His frown deepened. "Your affairs are now becoming embroiled with these Canadians."

"As my husband is a Canadian, I do not find this strange, Mr. Gardner."

"Canada is rife with Southern spies and sympathizers."

Ursula glanced out his windows as Marie Agathe and Henry appeared below. "As is this city, sir."

"Exactly. Seeking contacts. Drawing attention. To your household. To you."

She turned. "I would hasten to remind you that my family is steadfast to the Union cause, sir."

"Yes. The federal authorities have done you a great wrong in their past suspicions. They have lost your trail, and, I hope through our efforts, their interest. I only seek to keep you invisible. But the reclusive war widow Mrs. Major living modestly in Gramercy Park gathers attention of the larger world when she is visited by doting young soldiers. And when she consorts with a certain family of…actors."

Ursula laughed. "I easily disappear among the flamboyant Booths, sir!"

"I fear not, especially now that you are out of your widow's weeds."

She pivoted a circle with the remembered grace her dancing master had instilled in her feet. "Am I the image of a ravishing adventuress, then? With baby, hat askew and my bodice stained with Henry's milk?"

He grunted. "I know little of such matters."

She walked closer. "Oh, Mr. Gardner, you do not fool me for a moment. I see how your eyes alight when in our petit caneton's company. I shall keep to myself more, if this worries you. But you must extend your trust to my housekeeper and Henry's beloved Tante. Marie Agathe is our family."

Ursula realized that the document now in her solicitor's hand was a receipt from a recent purchase of ink, and not connected with the subject of their meeting at all. "Is that why this great show of bamboozlement regarding my inquiries about the Selby family, sir? You did not want to speak of them in front of Tante Marie Agathe?"

"Your father gave me a sacred charge, Mrs. Buckley," he said, dropping the receipt on his desk with a grunt. He used her real name, the legal one granted her once she had married Rowan. How did it still sound foreign to her ears? Was her marriage only a wonderful dream embedded in these war sorrows?

Ursula smiled, reaching for his hand there across the wide desk's surface. "My dear Mr. Gardner. I have made a good choice in husband, have I not?"

"I would have him ten years older. And bearded. With a few investments besides his confounded penny whistle. Furthermore, I fail to see how he required three women to raise him to manhood."

She laughed. "And you like my brother Jon as well, for all your complaining that he is as flighty as I am serious."

"He is your half brother. And has no ties whatsoever to your father's inheritance."

"He knows this sir. But he is our mother's child, and much loved by us both. Does his good past management of Fenwick Pines and his enlistment not improve your opinion of him?"

"It is not he, but his father—"

"Let us not speak of that man."

He sighed. "As you wish, Ursula."

What had it taken for him to use her given name? Do not you speak it so infused with pity, sir, she wanted to tell him. Instead, help me figure a way to assist the widow and daughter of a very different man—a man who had showed her nothing but kindness. But she could not hurt her counselor's feelings with a rebuke.

Did Mr. Gardner even sense the extent of Magnus Kingsley's crimes against her? No, only Miriam and her children knew. As enslaved people, they were used to treading in shadows, and secrets. They understood how she must keep these things hidden from Jonathan, from Rowan. Because knowing could lead to the ruination of them all. What would her men do with the knowledge? Jonathan's love was unshakable, but he would hate himself. And what of her Rowan? He had opened her world. He had even given her a child to love more than life itself. Would their Henry be enough to spread his love to her, or would he despise her and see their child as tainted too? Well, she must continue on her path to earn Rowan's love. Of her, not the paragon he thought her to be. He must not hate her. And he must never pity her. She could survive neither.

She made herself smile. A wide, bright, unnatural smile, she knew, but depended on her solicitor's poor eyesight not to see this. "And, think on it, next summer I will achieve my thirtieth year and so, in accordance with my father's will, you will be released from the great burden I am to you."

Mr. Gardner stared at their clasped hands. "I desire no such release," he said quietly.

"Then I shall not let you go. Neither will my too young, bare-faced menfolk."

Ursula finally sat at the chair he'd set out for her before his desk. "Now. To the matter at hand. Is my brother correct? Did our dear peddler Mr. Aaron Shulmann become Thomas Selby, dry goods merchant?"

"Yes. This is not unusual. It is a tradition of resourceful Jewish peddlers throughout the South. To earn enough to invest in this city where their goods originated."

"But why did he change his family's name?"

"Oh, that." His eyes scanned the papers on his desk. "It was already on a sign. A very handsome painted sign, from a generation ago, belonging to a merchant who packed up his wares and headed for California to provide for gold miners."

"My. How colorful."

His face brightened. "Yes! Just so. The sign had been stored in the cellar of the property. Painted by an itinerant artist, an immigrant who advanced in life to become a landscape artist of some note, I understand, from those who follow such things."

"I follow such things! What artist?"

"Cole."

"Thomas Cole?"

"Yes, I believe so."

"Why, Mr. Gardner, the paintings of Thomas Cole are renowned!"

"I prefer Church."

"Thomas Cole taught Frederic Church!"

"Is that so?"

"My father knew Thomas Cole. His own maritime paintings were influenced by him!"

"Well, perhaps that is how your father came by owning the property that housed the sign and asked me to purchase it for him."

"I have no doubt! Oh, this is a wonderful connection!"

"I'm afraid you must not pull this artist into your social circle if he can connect you to your father."

"Oh, that is hardly possible, as Thomas Cole died when still a young man, as my father did, many years ago."

"Oh, I see. A sad connection between them, then."

"Yes."

"So it will be no surprise to you—the decision by the peddler to preserve the sign intact. An eye for beauty Mr. Shulmann had, his widow is ample proof of that."

"I have not met the lady. But I see beauty in their daughter."

His face clouded. "The daughter, yes. Headstrong girl."

Ursula laughed. "You are thriving among many headstrong women, Mr. Gardner. And yet you only fear Marie Agathe, as shy and mild a lady as has ever taken the breath of life. This conversation has taken an odd turn."

"Yes, well. The simple fact is, Mr. Shulmann did not see the point of wasting a perfectly serviceable sign."

"So he changed his own name to that of the merchant for gold miners?"

Her solicitor's voice took on an odd quiver, even as it softened. "My dear lady. The sign was more than a sign. It was an opportunity for the family to achieve a new start here in this city. Mr. Shulmann's wife is Christian, and he did not require her to convert to a faith whose precepts he himself did not follow except in traditions."

"Like abstaining from pork. I see."

"I'm sure you are familiar with the fear and prejudice often directed at our Jewish friends. The daughter favors her mother in her... complexion. This family only desired a way to make their way in the world, and to be left in peace."

"And I disrupted their peace."

"Not at all! The rioters who threw this city into mayhem did that."

"But, before. I took their first home away from them."

"They had already settled in their new rooms, remember? A finer dwelling, without a leaking roof. And when I proposed that they remain at the same rent, they were most agreeable."

"They? Or Mr. Selby?"

"He spoke for the family, Madame!"

He only called her Madame when he was out of patience with her. "Of course, you are right. But now the family has lost Mr. Selby, who was our dear Mr. Shulmann, because he was brave enough to try and save another outsider from the rioters. His daughter is stealing into our garden, the one that she and her mother planted. I cannot help but feel that I have set unfortunate events into motion."

His smile was tight. "None of this rests on your shoulders. I have been remiss in my duties. My deepest apologies, Mrs. Buckley. I will be happy to see to the complete material comfort of Mr. Selby's widow and orphan. You need not think on them further."

Chapter Five ~ Rowan

"With that I was summarily dismissed, Jon," Ursula told her brother.

Rowan watched the two siblings' heads gravitate toward each other. Ursula's light brown tresses sparked with the same golden tones that shone throughout her brother's mane.

"Dismissed? How dare the man! I shall—" Jonathan reached for the hilt of a weapon that he seemed to forget was not slung to his side but hanging on a peg on the kitchen's stone wall next to Marie Agathe's market basket.

"No brandishing of your sword when we need to put our heads together and solve this interesting conundrum," his more level-leaded sister warned. "The fact remains that I did not think of this family enough. Surely Mr. Gardner, who has been so kind to me, could see that."

"Hmm, it is perplexing," her brother agreed. "What harm is there in allowing the child to harvest a few herbs?"

"Do not call our Penina a child. I was roundly rebuked for doing so."

"How dare the little snippet."

"Oh, you thought me quite grown up when I had achieved her years."

"Well, I was but half your age. And you both towered and lorded over me back then."

Rowan grinned as he held Baby Henry to his shoulder and paced the cobblestone floor of the kitchen. The siblings spoke of days gone by as they tried to solve their current dilemma— welcoming Ursula's latest stray over her lawyer's objections about any further contact with the Selbys.

He knew Mr. Gardner would not achieve his goal. Ursula was determined to expand their family. The "our Penina" gave her away. And he was sure Selby's widow would come with her orphan into his wife's fold soon enough.

Well, at least they were not actors.

Rowan loved watching the two Kingsleys like this, it reminded him of the love he bore his own closest sibling. If the Great Hunger had not robbed her of a future, perhaps Talitha would have children now, playmates for Henry, one day conspiring against their hapless parents together. For now, ah, it was a fine thing—their fledgling was falling asleep in his arms, lulled by his mother and uncle's voices, and the swaying walk Rowan modeled after the one his own father had perfected with the babies. Perhaps Rowan should teach the walk to their stray, 'our Penina,' so she could make herself useful with Baby.

So many ghosts guiding this family, he thought.

"What are you looking so self-satisfied about?" Jonathan demanded of him now. "It was I who held onto our little scamp's hands so he could toddle about the whole neighborhood greenery paths chasing robins. I need that nap more than he does!"

Ursula laughed as her brother's counterfeit scowl deepened. At times the man seemed to exist to make her laugh. Well, truth be told, they both took great pleasure in the pursuit, Rowan realized. Why was that? Even the baby he transferred into her arms let out a belch and a smile to keep his mother amused, it seemed.

Because the sadness in her eyes never left her.

When she returned from tucking him into the cradle in the small room behind the kitchen's fireplace, her eyes were swollen. She had been crying, again.

"How will I manage without you?" she whispered before he could ask the cause.

"Quite well, as always," he assured her, reaching for his pack by the door.

"And we will steal back on our next leave, for I cannot do without Marie Agathe's tourtiere," Jonathan added, kissing her cheek. "Even if we cannot find the proper grade of beef to make it 'a la mode Marie Catherine, still on the farm.'"

Rowan was grateful for her brother's humor then, masking what they both felt: fear for her and Henry every time they took their leave. Their visits fueled rumors that her widow's status did not allay among some of her neighbors. Those same neighbors delighted in telling their story: that of being assigned to protect Gramercy Park from the violence of last summer's Draft Riots and arriving to fulfill a very different duty: assisting at her birthing and welcoming Henry into the world. Now the gossips, they wondered why this Southern woman had such frequent visits from those two Yankee soldiers. Why had he and Jonathan not resumed their duties with her note of thanks? Why had they become friends and doting uncles to the widow's child?

Her growing friendships with the free-living writers, artists and actors of her neighborhood did not help her reputation either. And they were the most curious gossips of all.

Her fellow Marylanders, the Booths, were the worst of that lot. All but Edwin Booth were suspected of being southern sympathizers. Edwin's youngest brother, John Wilkes Booth, who often visited, was openly hostile. He often assured Rowan and Jonathan that there was no need to be so solicitous toward Ursula and her baby when there were so many other delights that the city could offer federal officers on leave. Especially them, who were turning negroes into soldiers on Rikers Island. He even suggested they could be carrying diseases from "filthy contrabands." As if the loyal, brave men that trained under his command were less than human. As if Rowan would ever imperil his wife and son!

But it was Edwin, the handsome widower Booth with the little daughter playmate for Henry, who most worried him. For Rowan could not fault in the man's word or deed. Edwin was intense and serious but showed no signs of the madness some said afflicted the family. He was even a reformed drunkard who now indulged himself only in vast quantities of coffee and cigars. And the Edwin Booth's appreciation of Ursula ran deep.

Rowan faced the bracing wind coming off the ferry's port bow. "We should invite Ursula and our Henry to our next drill and dress parade," he said.

Jonathan's initial delight tempered. "She would need an Army pass."

"Yes. And she is known only as our friend Mrs. Major, widow. Not your sister, not my wife. Just her doting admirers."

"Listen to me. I am as overjoyed as you that we have found my sister since she made her unscheduled departure from Maryland. But Ursula is in hiding. Your wife is still regarded as a spy for the Southern cause. And runaway spies can be shot. Until we can clear her name, we must remain vigilant."

"What if we tuck her within a church or charity group?"

Jonathan adjusted his hat to a decidedly unregulation casual angle, before folding his arms. "Well. I will consider that."

"Thank you."

"You're welcome."

"Jonathan. You do remember it is I who am your superior officer?"

"Now, I cannot help the bad judgement of the Army, can I?"

Chapter Six ~ Ursula

Ursula had not returned to this part of the city since the riots. Much of it was transformed, with the burned down wooden structures being replaced. She must ask Mr. Gardner if the repairs and rebuilding were being made by long term owners, or speculators. If she owned any of this block, she would insist on brick all around, and wide alleyways. She wondered who owned the Thomas Selby Mercantile building, now a quiet, half charred wooden hulk of three stories with new construction going on all around it.

She pushed open the door. There was the sign, lying on its side, beneath broken windows.

"What is your business here?" came a gruff voice from the shadows.

Ursula didn't recognize him at first, stooped and using a cane. And out of uniform. Her singing, dancing policeman. The one to whom she owed her life when he showed the path out of the madness that was the torching of the Spacious Firmament Orphan's Asylum.

"Sergeant Harrigan?"

"Bless my soul. Is it Mrs. Major, then?"

"Yes. And in one piece because of your good advice last summer. But you—oh, what happened? Did they storm the jail? The matron told me you were all safe!"

"Oh, we were. But my nieces, you remember them, Nan and Sary?"

"Our best teachers of the use of Mr. Singer's machine."

"Most kind of you to say so, Mrs. Major. Well, once Nan and Sary were both safe in police protection, they were terrified for their mother's life, and urged me to look after her. So I tried to cross town. To get my sister on a ferry over to Brooklyn. They knew who her at-sea sailor husband was, well not who he was, of course, but the tone of his skin you see, the mob did know. Oh aye...'Amalgamation, miscegenation, intermarriage—the sins that would surely seal the nation's doom!' so says the pamphlets, eh? I managed to see her off on the ferry, then thought I would check on you. Well, with all the smoke, I was disoriented. Here in my own city, imagine that? Somehow, I got to this street, where Mr. Selby's Dry

Goods store was on fire, and he was holding off a wild pack of rioters. I managed to drive them back long enough to get him off to the hospital in his women's care. The fire raged on. I tried to save that pretty sign, at least, from the flames. Then I was beset."

She touched the scorched sign. "You did," she breathed out. "You did save it."

"Aye. Almost." The elfin grin she remembered transformed his scarred face. "Thought I was done for and of no more use to anyone, lying there like a great hulk of rags. But the federal Army of these United States found me! Fresh from Gettysburg they were, good men. One from my own county in Ireland, imagine the miracle of that? I sent him and his lads to you, to Gramercy Park. Did they arrive?"

"They did indeed." Ursula pressed her gloved fingers against her mouth, realizing the role Sergeant Harrigan had played in reuniting her with her husband and brother. "Oh, you dear, dear man."

She did not trust herself to look into his concerned face, so she concentrated on the sign he lifted higher. The paintings on either side of the bold, clear lettering had no connection to what was inside the store. There were no buttons or silks, lanterns or gloves depicted. Somehow, she did not think that mattered a whit to the original Thomas Selby, because the images were so beautiful...a romantic rainbow framed meadow with wandering sheep amid a castle ruin on one side, and a moon kissed mountain scene on the other. Ursula's breathing finally evened out through the beauty of the damaged sign.

Sergeant Harrigan set the sign back down. "Mr. Cole was good, for an Englishman, was he not?"

She smiled at those merry eyes, framed by bushy brows the same ginger as his swept back curls. "Very good."

"Good enough for me to guard now, along with what's left inside from the vandals that still roam this street, looking to loot." He stole another glance under her wide-brimmed bonnet. "Are you well, Mrs. Major?" He glanced over her form. "And are you a mother, now?"

"I am. A fine boy named Henry Ryan after his grandfathers. He is napping, so I planned to meet Penina here to see the sign."

"Had that will o' the wisp told me to expect you I would not have been so gruff. You know the Selbys then?"

"A recent re-acquaintance," she said carefully.

"Well, that's grand."

"And you are...the empty bed," she realized.

"Ma'am?"

"The day Mr. Selby died, he was looking for you, in the bed beside his at the hospital."

"Was he, then?"

"My…my friend Sergeant Kingsley said he thought it signified that you had died."

"Oh no. We took sick together, that's true. Whenever a malady was going through the hospital, Mr. Selby and I seemed afflicted together. It was from the spoiled apples in the cobbler the night before. But I pulled though, and poor Thomas did not. They finished him off, those apples." He glanced down at his walking stick. "I am not able to remain on the police force, but I have been trying to look in on his women and what's left of their business since my sorry carcass was let go from the good hospital sisters' care."

"I would like to do the same for them, since I learned my need for a home caused the Selby Family's eviction the year before."

He smiled wide. "Now, there's a story in that, Mrs. Major."

Penina rounded the street, pulling a small wagon, her hair ribbons flying.

"Ah, I see you two have made introductions. Have you finished admiring Mr. Cole's fanciful painting, Mrs. Major?"

"I have."

"Good. Mother says to haul it home so she might store it properly and relieve Sergeant Harrigan of his guard duties. And she invites you both to condolence call tea. And my, I must do something to make that hat of yours more interesting, Mrs. Major! But first, I have struck a bargain with Abie's secondhand shop for a box of suspenders that is only scorched about the edges. Might you help me load it, Sergeant Harrigan?"

Ursula's slow smile was matched by that of the policeman's.

"Well. It looks like we are involved in another joint enterprise, Mrs. Major," he said, rolling up his sleeves.

The Selbys' house, only a short walk from the burned-out block of commercial buildings was indeed larger and more finely appointed than her own. From its bluestone stairs to rounded front entrance, it presented a picture of elegance. And the street was off the main shopping thoroughfare, and quiet.

"There's Mama," Penina announced.

Ursula saw an aproned woman dressed in simple black mourning standing in the doorway, waving. She was a head taller than her daughter and had a presence, from the warmth of her dark eyes to the wide smile, that was as welcoming as the rain of a sum-

53

mer's day. The hair that escaped the widow's simple silk snood was a mixed gray and brown, with a lovely wave before her ears.

Ursula hesitated on the bottom step, suddenly overwhelmed. She felt the gentle nudge of Sergeant Harrigan 's hand at the small of her back.

"You will enjoy each other's company," he said quietly at her ear. "You ladies share hearts that are golden, and true."

The woman took her hands in a strong grasp. "Thank you so much for coming, Mrs. Major. I am so happy to make your acquaintance and will not keep you longer than an hour's refreshment, after which I have arranged for a coach to return you to home and hearth."

"Might I go too, Mama? I love carriage rides and will have time to help Mrs. Major with her baby and in her garden before supper."

"Penina, you know better than to—"

Ursula laughed. "Penina will be very welcome in our garden after tea. I would dearly like her company and advice if you can spare her."

It was the news of a coach waiting that Ursula needed to hear, as she felt her bodice begin to tighten under her breasts. "Please accept my condolences," she began the visit.

"Thank you. I am so greatly in debt to both you and your household." She smiled at Ursula's companion. "And thank you for luring our Sergeant Harrigan away from his self-appointed duty at the store."

The policeman stepped forward now. "Mrs. Major and I are old friends, Mrs. Selby! And we have both been gainfully employed today, thanks to your diligent daughter."

Behind them, Ursula though she heard Penina's groan, but when she turned, the girl smiled wide. "Suspenders sold, Mama," she said.

Caroline Selby urged them all inside her home with a frank, easy charm.

Though sparsely furnished, its furniture and details were well chosen and placed. The tea was set out in the drawing room, its contents hot. How had she managed that, without servants? Beyond the slightly opened pocket doors, Ursula spied a room stacked with boxes smelling of the unmistakeable scent of fire.

As soon as Ursula sat next to the low tea table Penina whisked up behind her, a will of the wisp. She pulled the tie of Ursula's bonnet and removed it from her head. "I think this needs a pretty confection from my supplies. And more ribbons, of course," she said.

"Allow me to assist you Miss," Sergeant Harrigan implored, and they both disappeared down the hallway.

Caroline Selby shook her head. "This must seem a very strange notion of a condolence call, Mrs. Major."

Ursula took a sip of the invigorating tea. "A delightful variation."

"One my husband would heartily approve. He suffered greatly over these past months, but never complained. And he always sought to make us laugh. Penina tells me you have two such admirers in our Sergeant Kingsley and his captain."

"I do, indeed."

"Are we not the most fortunate of women?" She leaned forward and covered Ursula's hand with her own. "I believe you now know my husband's name was Aaron Shulmann before it became Thomas Selby. His end. It was so happy, Mrs. Major. I feel called to tell you this. Your Sergeant Kingsley came into our lives like, well, like an angel. And the memory of Aaron's long-ago exchange with Jonathan's sister brought my husband great peace in his last moments. If all might die as he did, death would be robbed of half its sting."

What did she give their dear Turtle Man back in that time? There were gaps in Ursula's memory. She held on to only brief images: Sister Raphaela's hands, her plants. Listening to the singing at matins, behind the grills smelling of frankincense. And before that, the hand of her father, guiding hers as she painted beside him, then that hand, too white, after he'd drowned at sea. And Munson's bloodhounds hunting human quarry.

"More tea, Mrs. Major?"

"Ursula, if you please?"

The older woman smiled broadly. "If I am Caroline to you."

Ursula nodded quickly, ashamed to show this beautiful, recently bereaved woman her tears. She was in Mrs. Shulmann's shadow, a sham widow, rich in extraordinary men who loved and cared for her.

Penina stood in the room's doorway, Ursula's more festooned hat in her hand. "Come, we must see to your baby, and then have time to plant in the cool of the day."

"Well. You have received your marching orders, Mrs. Major," Sergeant Harrigan, his red hair sporting a leftover feather from Penina's worktable, concluded.

When she heard Henry's cry from his napping station behind the kitchen hearth, Ursula took him up and brought him to her breast before she'd removed her wide-brimmed bonnet. As she rocked, he stared up at it, dancing his fingers to the breeze-swept ribbons. She caught Penina watching the process with something that resembled wonder.

Marie Agathe looked up from her sewing. "A good choice," she complimented their guest. "He likes the reds. And look, Baby has his father's sense of the rhythms, no?"

"Was your husband a musician then, Mrs. Major?" Penina asked.

Ursula exchanged a warning glance with a chastened Marie Agathe. "Yes," she answered carefully, the truth. "We used to play music together."

"Where?"

"Oh, not formally. In hospital wards." Yes, both at her motherhouse and in Washington. It helped to say it, to remember that she and Rowan shared a past, however brief its moments. They were building a history together. Perhaps theirs would become a real and true marriage.

Penina stood behind Ursula and deftly removed her bonnet. She brought its new cluster of decoration closer to the baby.

"You like what I have done, making your mother more fashionable, do you not, dear little—"

"Bird!" he chirped, sitting up and reaching for the silk black and white chickadee that peeked out from under the bonnet's rim.

"Mrs. Major! Did he say—?"

"His first word! Oh, Penina, you have inspired it, with your marvelous improvement!"

"An expression of the gas only," Marie Agathe maintained, tucking her lace trimmed shawl into her waistband. "I have been schooling him to say maman for some weeks now. That will be his first word."

Although they could not get him to repeat his accomplishment, the baby stroked the round silk bird's head, laughing before he returned to his mother's breast.

Once he was fed, Ursula carried Henry out with them to the garden. He did not desire his hands held for trotting about, for once. He seemed content to crawl around his mother and Penina as they worked in the soil. So Marie Agathe returned to the hearth room while he watched the breeze blow past the spring blooms, and reached for wood thrushes and sparrows that hopped or flew out of his reach.

"Does your baby have grandparents that visit?" the girl asked, as Ursula handed her an extra pair of garden gloves.

The truth, simply said. It was safe. "No dear. They are all gone from this life."

"And where are your soldiers?"

"They were called back to their duties."

"They do not like me."

She began delineating a row against the fencing for the peas. "Now, Penina, why do you believe so?"

"The Captain, he regards me coldly."

"How is this so?"

"It is difficult to explain. He appears a good man. He even seems interested in my thoughts, beyond trying to please you with this interest, I mean. But when he does not know I am watching, he looks through me, as if he wishes I were not there. Those strange eyes. The blue coldness of them sends chills up my arms."

"Captain Buckley was gravely injured at the battle of Antietam, dear. I believe what you observe at those times is his glass eye, which does not see you watching him, and cannot reflect the warmth of his heart."

"Oh. Oh, my. Truly?"

"Truly."

"Well, perhaps I am mistaken, then."

Henry crawled into the flowerbed and righted himself. Ursula handed him his amber bead teething necklace and he began chewing happily.

"Well, it may be that Sergeant Kingsley enjoys my company, a little," Penina said as they resumed their planting. "Though I cannot tell with the Southern-bred gentlemen, because they are so polite. We used to have many as our regular customers. They would tell my mama how beautiful is her smile today, and thank her for gracing our store with such a lovely daughter, Is that not prettily said?"

"Yes." Ursula thought of all the gentlemen who turned her own young head with such phrases.

"You want to say something more."

"Dear?"

"You dig harder in the garden when you want to say something more. And your jaw gets a little tight."

My. Penina Selby was an observant child.

Ursula smiled. "Would your mother want to share the climbing peas? Shall we plant more of them?"

"Oh yes—she prepares them both fresh and boiled. Papa likes them in—." She stopped herself abruptly. "Mother took me aside before we left our house. She says I am to be no trouble and only helpful. I promised to never again invite myself and only come when I am invited here. She says you are a dear lady who has suffered her own losses."

"And she is, to me, already a beacon of possibility in my own life as the mother of little Henry."

"Surely you do not want your baby to become as troublesome as I am?"

Ursula laughed. "Troublesome? No. Full of adventuring spirit, curiosity, resourcefulness! I should love for Henry to be under your sphere of influence. That would be his great fortune. And mine. To have your friendship, I mean. Have you made any judgement concerning that possibility, Penina?"

"Not yet." She looked out past the herbs to where Henry was inspecting a purple tulip. "But I like your baby."

"So do I."

Penina giggled. Ursula's heart swelled with the sound. Why? Why was it so important to her to be in the good graces of this ill-mannered girl?

"Why does Sergeant Kingsley call the baby "HRB?"

"They are the initial letters of his names. Henry and Ryan."

"But M is his surname's initial, is it not? For Major. Why are his initials not HRM?"

Ursula dug too deeply for the peas to ever find their way into the sunlight. "Why… why, HRH? That sounds too much like British royalty, so Sergeant Kingsley thought. Very unpatriotic in our democratic republic."

"But why choose—"

"We also call him Baby, so the letters became HRB."

The girl considered the explanation, as Ursula remembered to scold Jonathan for getting her into yet another predicament.

"I like it," Penina finally decided. "It's short, like him."

"Indeed!" Ursula laughed longer than the merit of the joke warranted, she was so relieved. And she was glad when, outside fascinations wearing thin, Henry reached out his arms for her.

"Ah, are we too late to join Baby Henry in his per-ambulations today?" a deep, rich voice sounded from the other side of the boxwood hedges.

Ursula stood. "Not at all Mr. Booth! I believe he had been patiently waiting for you and, is she there with you? Yes, his dearest little friend, Edwina! Will you help to guide him as he walks?" She lifted Henry so he might see over the hedge. Catching sight of the almost three-year-old year old in her father's arms, he squealed with glee.

The man removed his fashionable slouch hat. "And who is this new flower of your garden?"

"Penina Selby, sir, who is more than a flower. She is one of the originators of the beds that are home to medicinals that have soothed your throat this winter past. Penina Selby, may I present—"

"Edwin Booth," Penina finished breathlessly. "The foremost American Shakespearean actor of our age." She stood, the garden spade dropping into the peas' bed with a quiet sifting sound.

"My dear Mrs. Major," the tragedian proclaimed, laughing, "We must find Miss Selby a position as a theater reviewer at the New York Times."

Chapter Seven ~ Penina

Find your voice, she kept telling herself. But her tongue remained thick in her mouth as the widow chatted with Edwin Booth about the antics of their children. It was he: Edwin Booth, the man she'd only stolen glances at since she was a child.

"My father and I attended a performance when you played the Merchant of Venice," she blurted out, interrupting them.

The actor pushed his great black mane back from that high forehead that held so much poetry within and focused his intense dark eyes on her.

"Did you? This honors me."

"My father said only you among players have discovered the secret Shakespeare placed within the play: that *The Merchant of Venice* is Portia's comedy, but Shylock's tragedy."

"What a wonderful compliment."

"Yes. We read the play together before the performance, so that I would understand it better. He explained to me your make up did not include a hooked
nose or exaggerated features because you sought to
impart Shylock's humanity, his oppression, and the
oppression of his people. So that we might understand the reason he exacted such an awful price for
his loan. My father was of the Jewish people, you
see."

"Was he?"

"Yes. He said that you found how Shylock saw
himself as the guardian of the law. But he did not
temper his justice with mercy, Papa said. And that he
gave in to his greed, which placed the value of his
ducats over his own daughter. My papa would never
do that."

Edwin Booth stared at her with that same pene-
trating gaze that had held her transfixed, there in her
balcony seat. Her mouth went dry. What was she doing talking to the great actor in this way?

"And I believe your father and his own Jessica
were the best of attendants that evening. I visited
synagogues to help form my portrayal. I read the To-
rah and the Koran to teach myself the precepts and
principles of all three Abrahamic religions. The Bard
understood the deep recesses of the human heart,

Miss Selby, as I suspect you already know. We mere mortals must forever study to bring his creations to life.

"Well, now." He returned his attention to the widow. "What a wonderful new friend you have found, Mrs. Major."

He swept his hat across his body as he made a deep bow to them both.

His little daughter clapped her hands, and the baby happily followed her movements with his own chubby little fingers.

"Quite right, Edwina and Henry!" He laughed. "Bravo, to Miss Selby, Shakespearean scholar of the first water. Mrs. Major must include you in every musical interlude she provides our rehearsal henceforth. And kindly urge her to visit us more often so we can hear your notions on all things Shakespearian as well as her delightful Chopin and Liszt."

***

"I know I stayed longer than you advised, Mama," Penina said before she'd even removed her hat. "But oh, the result. Imagine Edwin Booth himself in our garden. And I was helpful there and with the baby, and even the French lady who is housekeeper and who I am sure thinks I talk much too much for a prop-

67

er child, sent me home with a slice of her dried apple cake for you."

"What a wonderful adventure."

"You are not angry?"

"No, dear. A little envious, I think."

"Why? Mrs. Major adores you."

"Surely not."

"She wants to be like you, she told me herself. She wishes her son to be as accomplished as I, and so," she threw her arms around her mother's neck, "she must become as fine a mother as you are, you see?"

"I am not sure one follows the other, my darling. And perhaps she has her own mother to guide her."

"No. Both her parents are deceased."

"Penina. You did not ask—"

"I did." She brought her mother to her favorite chair by the drawing room's fire and sat at her feet. "Mama, our Sergeant Kingsley has brought Mrs. Major into our lives in her own person, not Mr. Burwell's twice-told rumors about 'the widow' in our house. We must decide for ourselves if Mrs. Major is worthy of our friendship."

"Worthy? Penina, what a notion. The poor lady."

"Now that she is not. Poor, I mean. Though I doubt our mutual and very discreet landlord will ever impart to us the extent of her inheritance."

"And you must promise me to never even bring up that subject with either of them. Now let me bring out our suppers. I have my own wonderful news from Mr. Gardner that I must tell you this evening."

Chapter Eight ~ Ursula

"As Addison once observed, 'women are armed with fans as men with swords, and sometimes do more execution with them,'" John Wilkes Booth remarked, bowing before Ursula.

What had she done? Was she too obvious in her signaling to Miriam across the room that her part in the musicale was about to begin?

He laughed at her expression. "Oh, my dear lady, worry not! No one would suspect one such as you of treachery."

"Such as me?" she repeated. It was a bad habit she had now picked up from Rowan.

Adam Badeau clapped the actor's shoulder. "Nonsense. Always suspect the quiet ones," he said with a broad wink. "Oh, how we have missed you over your confinement and motherly dedication, dear lady."

John Wilkes shook him off. Never overly friendly with the family's friend, he'd taken an active dislike to him since Adam had recovered sufficiently to return to his new duty on General Grant's staff. Was it because Adam Badeau was rich and important enough to be open about being a man's man? Ursula hardly thought so, as such things were accepted in the drawing rooms of artists and actors, musicians and playwrights. It was one of the reasons she loved about being in their company. They were high-strung, fought and wounded each other extravagantly, but forgave easily too and were endlessly curious and affectionate, defying society's narrower precepts about where that curiosity and affections belonged.

And there were so many gaps in her own education she needed to fill. The artists and actors treated her as one of their own, and she did not feel as ignorant in their company.

Miriam nodded, then left the room, understanding, fetching Penina from the kitchen, where she was repairing Rosalie Booth's hair ornament. Good. They would walk home together once Ursula played the nocturne, Miriam collected her wages for supervising the hired out supper staff. Participation in Booth entertainments was becoming more like obligations. Ursula longed to have her baby in her arms, though she knew little Henry, much more sensible than his mother, was likely sleeping soundly.

Ursula felt the fissure between the two Booth brothers widening. It was not only because of Adam's effusive praise of Edwin's more natural acting style. Perhaps the older brother was more sought after on northern stages, but John Wilkes was the darling of critics of the south. A third, the oldest Booth brother Junius commanded the stages of the West. But Edwin was clearly the head of his large family, while their widowed mother was its heart.

Miriam had a harsher view of the family's doted on youngest brother. "That one, he spoiled like winter apple. Pretty on the outside but take a sniff. Hiding rotten, Miss Ursula," she had confided.

Edwin was a Unionist. And Adam Badeau was now on General Grant's staff. Asia, Rosalie and their mother strove to be a neural force between opposing views, but Miriam was right as usual, John Wilkes was clearly their favorite, and much indulged. Perhaps when Junius arrived from San Francisco to perform their long planned benefit performance together, he would help bring harmony to the fractured family.

"Ah, perfection," Rosalie proclaimed, taking the ornament from Penina's hand. Her sister Asia agreed. "Better than it was before. What have you done, child?"

Ursula noticed that Penina did not bristle with offense, as she would have if a 'child' had slipped from her own lips.

"Why, only a little ribbon, curled in the French style, Mrs. Clark. Oh, and I mingled in a few leaves and blossoms of white jasmine."

Asia turned to her. "Ursula, where on earth did you find this treasure?"

"She was your neighbor here in Gramercy Park before I was."

"The Selbys? The mercantile Selbys? Of course. How were we never introduced?"

Ursula smiled. "This is a mystery to me as well."

"Well, we must make up for the grievous oversight. You are now our darling Penina, and, as such, when are you going to have your parents release you from that dear but commonplace store to establish your own millinery?"

Oh, no. The Booths, and especially Asia and Rosalie, were not going to swallow Penina up whole. Ursula did not know what precisely a millinery was, but she determined to find out.

Chapter Nine ~ Rowan

"My." She blinked in that delightful, surprised way of hers. "That was… refreshing."

"Is that what I am, wife? An invigoration? Like a crisp apple ripened in the sun?"

"More like a peach."

He felt her buttocks tighten there, in his hands, and laughed. It was his overindulgence with a peach flavored intoxicant that had gotten them started, after all. And her guiding hands. For the first time they had loved each other, he was wounded, blind and given up for dead in a Maryland convent turned hospital. He breathed deeply of her scent. It was crisp linen and her medicinals back then. Now it was the blue-tinged milk from fulsome breasts, her garden's greens, and under it all, the cigar smoke of Edwin Booth's parlor.

Expensive cigars, like the ones his Army superiors smoked, when they came into camp to berate him.

Stop it. Do not allow either the Booths or his superiors to poison this time with her.

Rowan swung his legs off the side of her bed. Ursula sighed deeply, signaling her slip into contented drowsiness. Good, let her rest so he could remove the membrane. Upon Marie Agathe's instruction, Jonathan had procured a supply from a chemist's shop near the Five Points brothels.

Who knows how long this war would continue, how long it would take them to free Ursula's good name of the charges of sedition made against her? Henry was accepted as a recently widowed woman's offspring. Another baby would not be. Both Marie Agathe and Jonathan had hammered that into him. But Rowan also knew Ursula did not consider their marriage yet made in the highest order, before God, despite their chapel wedding, before a priest.

"Rowan." Ursula's suddenly melancholy tone startled him. "You do not find the joy that I do in our intimacy."

"Of course I do."

"You need not hide what you are doing. Marie Agathe told me what they were. And she said that, because of wearing them, you would not find as much pleasure as…before Henry."

"Marie Agathe is a single lady who has chosen a celibate life. What does she know of men's pleasure?"

"Do not you try that Irish trick of answering with questions. She has warned me of that too."

There were tears in her eyes. He slipped back under the covers and took her into his arms. "'Sula, listen to me now. We must take care of you, Henry and I." There. She was leaning against his heart. "Our little nursling is still keeping your courses from returning, is he not?"

"Yes."

"As he should, to keep you well, and not overworn with childbearing." He kissed the crown of her delightfully disheveled gold brown hair. "But he is now taking a few bits of potato, and a little mashed apple off his baby spoon, too. Your courses will return as he takes less of your milk. My own mother would have my head on a platter if I did not do my share to make sure our children came far enough apart to preserve your health and the joy we take in them."

"Did her own children come that way, Rowan? Apart?"

"At least three years between for all five of us. We were champions at the feeding."

She laughed, but in a way that broke his heart. "Five. You have told me only of Talitha. Five? What were their names?"

"Mam presented our da with Aoife, Niall, Talitha, myself, and the baby Ciara. Only Talitha and I lived long enough to board the ship for Canada with them."

"Oh, Rowan."

"Do not you, 'Oh, Rowan,' me, woman. Look now, you are leaking everywhere, and our Henry will have no milk this morning."

She wiped her eyes. "You have had other women." Good God, Rowan thought, she was shifting tack like her sailor father now. "They have known how to please you better than I at… at the plowing."

"The plowing?"

"It is what Marie Agathe calls what we do."

Rowan was beginning to wish the three sisters who raised him on their farm in Quebec since the age of five had sent Marie Catherine, who was not as good with babies, but better at the pies. He stared down his wife with narrowed eye. "And do you think all men are such shallow creatures that have but one form of delight?"

"Another question, is it?"

"Why are you plaguing me?"

"And another!"

Tabernac, but he was enjoying even the fighting with her. And he was hard again. She saw, and laughed, even with tears still wet on her cheeks.

His steady, constant Ursula had grown so mercurial since giving birth.

He growled like a bear. "My condition amuses? You see before you a desperate man, wife."

"And you see a woman blessed in the vigor of her husband," she said, not raising those sparked-with-gold eyes to his. But he saw signs at her cheeks, at those erect, begging-to-be-kissed nipples. He was glad Marie Agathe had insisted on a good supply of the sheaths. He would need more. He reached for his coat pocket. No need to hide them from her now.

She looked over his shoulder. "From what is it made?"

Ursula, the curious scientist she was, again. "Animal bladder."

"What animal?"

"Sheep."

"How very resourceful. And so tight a fit. It does not hurt you?"

"No, love."

Her lips were at his ear now. "Might I help you put it on, my shepherd?" she whispered.

"Only if you seek to add to my shallow delight in you."

"Oh, I do!"

How he wished she had spoken their wedding vows with such enthusiasm.

"Remind me to steal all my wives out of convents," he said, to make her laugh.

She did, and he was heartily glad she was draped only in her bed's sheet.

***

Rowan dressed and slipped out of the room while she was sleeping. When he entered the kitchen, Marie Agathe was already stirring the oats. The most meticulous of the Canadian sisters who raised him, she, of course, noted his buttoned-in-the-dark vest.

"Passe la nuit sur la corde à linge?" she asked if he had been awake all night.

"Mais non," he insisted. "We are well rested, both."

He received a sly wink, reminding him of Marie Madeline, the many times married sister who now ruled Ursula's Maryland estate and probably the Union soldiers quartered there as well. "You know how to keep your woman's back from the cold, eh?"

Rowan tried hard to look offended at yet another remark directed at his shallow pleasures. "J'ai trouvé l'amour de ma vie," he proclaimed is devotion to Ursula as the love of his life. "Why would I not want to please her in every way?"

"Tu es un beau parleur!" she scoffed him as a smooth talker.

He frowned. "And your English, Tante Marie Agathe? It is not so smooth. Let us stay within its boundaries to improve, eh?"

She did not look properly chastised, but at least more serious. "Oui... good. Now then, what is the trouble between you and your wife, petit frere?"

"Did I say—?"

"Do not question what I see in your eyes, Rowan Buckley." She raised herself to her full height, which matched his own. All the sisters were tall, making him think Canada was a land of giants when he'd first stumbled into their barn as a five year old runaway from the typhus wards on Grosse Isle. She saw through his bluster then as she did now. "You think because I do not have the English language so well that I will allow this always questions trick of the Irish?"

He grinned. "The both of you, now?"

Made speechless by her anger, she held up one finger. It was a little bent, crippled by a lifetime of work with heavy ironware. Do not show it, his fear of his Maries aging, of leaving him.

Success. She handed him his morning coffee with only a grunt.

"Merci."

"En Anglais." she admonished him primly, smoothing her iron grey hair under her embroidered cap.

He surrendered. "Marie Agathe, why does she cry all the time?"

"Your Ursula, she is a good, practical girl, no? She birthed into the world a baby, your baby. She now gives nourishment from her body. This is a time sensitive. Her feelings are close to…how do you put it in the English? Her sleeve?"

"She is not unhappy with me?"

"You men! You think all of the life of the woman tourne …oh, what is the English?"

"Revolves."

"Yes—revolves around you?"

"Ursula has pursuits. She has had them always. Even when she was a holy sister, her life was her garden, and her healing. Here in this vast city, she has a crafty lawyer looking after her, procuring things that make her comfortable, and her beautiful piano. And she has friends, so many friends of all colors and stations in the life of this city, who would gladly put their hands in the fire for her. And now this little girl, her stray."

"You are not eaten with the envy of her petite orphan, surely?"

"No, no! But Ursula's inheritance has granted her independence, and duties. Marie Agathe, I am so small a part of her life."

"Your own choices have dictated this, Captain Buckley."

His enlistment in the Americans' war was an old wound between himself and the blunt Canadian sisters who had mothered him after his parents were consigned to their mid-Atlantic graves. "Of course, you are right," he conceded. "But I try to look after Ursula's brother. Will this help do you think?"

"Help with what?"

"With her wishing to be my wife."

"She is your wife, Rowan."

He frowned. Out with it. "We made an agreement. To decide after the war."

"Decide? What is there to decide? You pronounced your vows in a church, before God. Marie Madeline made sure of this, when you were down in Mary's Land."

"But it was to save her from prison, or a spy's death that we married. Marie Agathe, look at me! Why would she want to stay with an ignorant, broken-down soldier, when she has her own fortune? When she has admirers at every turn of her skirts?"

Marie Agathe was silent, her light eyes searching his face. Had she not understood him? Perhaps he was picking up the habit of the New Yorkers: speaking too quickly.

Finally, she shook her head. "You are serious. You, who have walked through the fires of hell with her, for her. You enjoy each other in the pleasures of the bed. You have a beautiful child together. Yet you are afraid she will leave you?"

"Of course I am afraid. Mais bien sûr."

"My darling boy. La belle dame is innocent in many of the ways of the world, perhaps. And in the strength of her woman's power. But your Ursula, she is not a stupid woman. Now get out of my kitchen with your troubles of the imagining, I have work to do."

"You sound like Marie Madeline," he groused.

"You need less of my coddling, maybe. You require some of Marie Madeline's impatience with your notions, maybe." She looked him over as if he was one of her Cochin China roosters. "And some of Marie Catherine's cooking on your bones. Oh, where are my sisters? I cannot do everything. Pars tant que tu le peux. Go!"

His wife stood in the kitchen doorway. "I thought only Jonathan could invoke our Marie Agathe's wrath to this degree," she observed.

"Your brother, he is the Angel Gabriel next to this one," Marie Agathe complained, taking the stack of linens from Ursula's arms. Leaving them open.

For him.

He took her waist between his hands and kissed her. Because he was not a stupid man.

He only allowed her a startled breath before he pulled her closer and did it again. There, that little stumble against him that was her body's habit when her knees went weak.

"My." Ursula breathed out. "You two must argue more often."

That dimple. He was undone.

He lifted her into his arms and climbed the back stairs toward her bedroom. There was time. Marie Agathe had not yet cracked an egg. And Jonathan would hold the ferryman with a bribe.

Chapter Ten ~ Ursula

Rikers Island, New York City
Sunday, May 8, 1864

Their audience stood at respectful attention. The children's small flags still waved, but only responding to the breezes coming off the East River. The drumming started and Rowan nodded to his sergeants, Jonathan and Sling among them. They began to call out formations. In his little cart, Henry slept though it all.

"Does it not make you uneasy, Mrs. Major?" Penina whispered beside her.

"What. dear?"

"The rifles. I mean, at their shoulders."

"They are soldiers. And we are at war."

"But they must be very angry. At all white people. And after the events of last summer, here in this city. Our tenant Mr. Burwell once warned us that it might be enough anger to foment an insurrection. Black against white. That they would turn those guns and slaughter us all."

Ursula felt her jaw tighten. She hoped she never had the pleasure of meeting their seldom-seen tenant, for she feared she might do the man physical harm for frightening a fatherless child.

"War is a terrible thing. We are fighting an insurrection begun by the southern states. With the help of these determined and sacrificing men we will prevail and knit our country back together again."

"Mr. Burwell says you are under the influence of your admirers."

"I am under the influence of the circumstances and events of my life, Penina."

"Well. Papa always said we must treat all as children of God."

"I think your papa was a wise man."

"Sergeant Kingsley was acquainted with him. Do you know that?"

Ursula's fingers clutched the edge of her shawl. She must be careful. "I do."

"And his sister was, too."

"So I understand."

"It's strange, is it not? That we have found each other here in this city of a million people?"

"Strange and wonderful."

"Like a gift from God?"

"Exactly."

"But Mr. Burwell says we were born in sin and must come to redemption. Does that philosophy have room for undeserved gifts?"

Mr. Burwell, again. How much time had their tenant spent with a lonely, frightened child? A child with a grievously injured father, languishing for months. With a mother caring for him while struggling to salvage a business. Why was their tenant so generous with his attention? Penina's Mr. Burwell did not sound like a generous man.

The drumming stopped. Rowan ordered the men to take their ease. The small flags began waving wildly in time to the clapping and cheers. Wide smiles broke out all around.

Her men looked so handsome in their dress uniforms, as did their platoons. Unlike the separations quickly made with other officers, Sling and his men reached out to her husband and brother, even while surrounded by their own family and friends. They talked, shook hands, made introductions to their island's visitors. These men were lighting the way to a brighter future for the country, when the war was over. It was a day of gifts.

The dress parade was over. Time to get to work.

The wide tents the soldiers had set up for the weekly visit of the Union League Club, St. Benedict the Moor parish, Abyssinian Baptist Church, and the Cooper Union craftsmen had sides pinned back to take advantage of the summer breeze. Mrs. Gibbons, though burned out of her own house in the draft rioting last year, walked among the tables, welcoming her recruits, Ursula and the Selbys among them. But it was mostly accomplished free people of color who visited and worked with the soldiers—carpenters, joiners, rope makers and schoolteachers from Weeksville.

Outside the tents, the Downing family of Oyster House fame was cooking up an open fire pot of seafood stew. Out on the shore, several of the Downings were admiring herons and showing the soldiers how to dig for and shuck oysters.

How Ursula wished the rest of the city of New York could see the beauty of this day, of the strength and fortitude of these men, willing to die for the country that had enslaved them, that offered them only promises of a better future for themselves and their families.

Caroline Selby had all but emptied her peddler's hand cart of paper flower bouquets and small fans—

penny gifts for the soldiers' mothers and sisters and sweethearts who had come on visitors' day.

Ursula slowed the little back and forth pushes of the wheeled cart that the carpenter and carriage maker squads had fashioned for Henry's visits. He shifted to his side and pillowed his head with his arm, exactly as his father did when heading into a deeper sleep. The sight caught her breath. How wonderful that she knew such a thing. Was there hope for them as a family? Was there a future?

Tears threatened, yet again, and she was glad for the sight of Caroline Selby's black skirts finding a place beside her on the bench. Together they watched Penina's head down beside the drummer's, encouraging his slate work in arithmetic.

"She has her father's instincts with the trade, but she can use them for this, more worthy and lasting occupation, can she not, Ursula?"

"Indeed. I learned of young Tate's service after Gettysburg. Oh, Caroline, he saw things that no one of his years should see when he was working with the gravediggers. He would barely speak when first he came to his duties, Captain Buckley said. It was Penina who finally got him to venture inside our litera-cy tent today. And now, look, he practices his sums, and writes his name."

"I think Penina hides behind her frivolity."

"I do not see her as overly frivolous, Caroline."

"I am glad to hear you say so. For I would not want you living with the impression that she cannot ponder deeply, or that she lacks a generous nature." Caroline folded her hands. "Or that she does not suffer the loss of her father."

"Perhaps Penina and I are not yet devout enough friends for her to express some of her deeper emotions."

"I hope that time will come."

"If she can forgive me."

"Forgive you?"

"For taking up residence in your home without seeking your permission."

Caroline Selby let out a quick burst of laughter, then stifled it when Henry stirred in his little cart. "Our landlord Mr. Gardner had our permission."

"But my arrival in New York caused the loss of your home, your garden."

"Gramercy Park is a lovely setting. But oh, Ursula, you have called on us. You have seen how fine a dwelling ours is. Why, Penina danced about the larger rooms with their elegant trappings and high ceilings when first we arrived. Its location closer to our shop allowed more time with her dear papa. Yes, she missed the garden. But I do not know how we might have paid the rent after the riots. There our home came to our aid as well. It was large enough that, after we lost so many of our shop's goods to the fire, we could offer an entire three rooms to a tenant."

"Your Mr. Burwell."

"Oh, never my Mr. Burwell. Most especially since I learned the man was fueling Penina's resentment toward you, a war widow who deserved so much more respect and privacy as you make your way in the world. Even my Aaron urged me to throw the man out and offer the rooms to Sergeant Harrigan."

"What a splendid idea. Have you done so?"

"I was working up the courage when Mr. Burwell informed me of more important business in Canada that might keep him for an extended time. He put two month's rent into my hands and flew out the door. Our own need got the better of me, I'm afraid. I decided to wait for his return."

"Yes," Ursula decided. "I would have done the same."

"But how dare he take advantage of my daughter's longing for our plantings and the quiet walkways of Gramercy Park? He'll get no letter of recommendation from me. Penina has come under better influences. And now, we have an entire plot of our own, thanks to our Mr. Gardner."

"Mr. Gardner?"

"Indeed, yes. Our dear common landlord has purchased the green lot behind our home and asked us to maintain it. Might I be correct in supposing that you have planted the idea in his head?"

"Hmmn."

"He has enclosed it in a fine iron fence, with a gate. It contains herbal as well as flower and fruit gardens and even a small orchard of cherry trees. And the cost to us? Why, he has reduced our rent in return for a bushel of cherries come summer. Imagine."

"I can well imagine."

"Is he not the most generous of men?"

Why was she bothered by Caroline Selby and her daughter not knowing their actual benefactor? "I expect Penina will be busy there."

Caroline's burst of laughter surprised her. "That is what Mr. Gardner said, his very words. But so sternly voiced, as if the garden is our obligation, instead of a place of haven and delight."

"I enjoy cherries, too." Ursula frowned. Now she was sounding as petulant as Penina. Or herself at fourteen.

Caroline patted her hand. "And you shall have as many as your heart desires. Do you think Penina and I will abandon you now?"

"You have reason to, now that you have your own garden." She still sounded too much like her younger self. What was wrong with her?

"Oh, my dear Ursula, after all your kindnesses? And introducing us to the good work of this society, so that we may be useful to these brave soldiers and their families? All this, besides enjoying Sunday afternoons out in the more healthful air of this island? And I must admit another reason to be thankful."

"Oh?"

"You have also introduced us to the fashionable folks that the Booth family know. They seem to desire hats and bonnets as lovely as yours." She took hold of Ursula's hands. "We women should keep making alliances with each other. Are they not most beneficial?"

Ursula felt a surge of holy possibility. It was much like the one she felt when Sister Raphaela took notice of her efforts in the garden, and when she'd met two out of three of Rowan's Marie Madeline and Marie Agathe, and they decided she was worthy of him.

"Mrs. Major, you have been so kind to us, and patient with Penina, her mercurial disposition," the older woman continued as she picked up a paper rose and attached it to a wire stem, "And her incessant match-making. It comes from offering wares in this city, I'm afraid, where even affairs of the heart are often seen through transactional eyes."

Ursula shook her head in amusement. "I hear you are also plagued by her efforts."

Caroline Selby glanced down at her lap, growing with blue roses. A hint of a blush rose to her cheeks.

Ursula smiled. "I am firm in the belief that Sergeant Harrigan is a fine man."

"Indeed he is. And he kept Mr. Selby good company at the hospital though both were suffering."

"Have you and Penina met his family?" Ursula asked carefully, easing a small kink in a paper fan.

"We have. He resides with his sister and her children. They regard each other in a most tender way, and he, even in his crippled condition, provides a measure of protection while her husband is out to sea. We enjoy their visits to our home and have paid call on them as well."

"How wonderful. How perfectly splendid."

Ursula felt a wave of elation. She thought of her Sergeant's nieces who sewed clothes for the orphans and whose sailor father was a negro.

"You need not be concerned," Caroline added, as if hearing her thoughts, "I was disowned by my own family and shunned by my church for marrying a Jewish peddler man. It made no difference that he was a welcome guest to our home when on his rounds."

Caroline Selby was an extraordinary woman, Ursula decided. One more reason to be happy that Mr. Gardner had found ways to make her life more secure. It did not matter that she and Penina saw him as their protector, and not her. It did not matter at all.

"Caroline, perhaps we should invite Sergeant Harrigan and his sister's family to join us here on the island next time? He is wonderful at gathering up children with his stories, and he has a beautiful singing voice."

"I am sure they would enjoy this place," her friend agreed. "But, my friend, remember: it is too soon for me to think of marriage."

"Well," Ursula added a fan to its basket, "it is good that Sergeant Harrigan is a patient man."

"Now you sound like Penina."

"Do I?"

Caroline's smile softened. "My husband and I had many wonderful years together, made better still once Penina joined us. Aaron resided at the center of my heart for many years."

"And so he would wish for you to be happy and secure."

Caroline emptied her apron of flowers onto the spread cloth at their feet. "Sergeant Harrigan is a decade younger than I."

"Truly? And yet old enough to be discerning in women."

"Indeed."

The older woman grinned wide now. Ursula felt she was about to learn a delicious secret. "Do you know, he has admitted to me that he was always happy in your own presence? Though he never had the courage to even ask your given name."

"Why ever not?"

"Because you were friends, but you always seemed married, he told me, despite the black you wore over your year of mourning. He would watch you sometimes, standing with your cup of afternoon tea, pouring over the newspapers he would deliver to the orphanage. You read the names of the latest dead and wounded, as if you were not already widowed."

"My."

The embodiment of one of the names she had searched the papers for, Jonathan, swept by, depositing two glasses of lemonade into their hands before he opened the canvas covered camp stool he'd tucked under his arm.

"Drink. And keep those feet up, it is a warm day," he demanded, lifting Ursula's heels until they rested on the stool. He took a quick glance at the sleeping baby, backed away one step and tipped his Hardee hat that now had a black ostrich feather tucked into its folded up left side. "Penina's latest creation," he admitted with a glance in the girl's direction. "She says it reveals me as a seeker of truth and wisdom. Ladies," he excused himself, before disappearing.

"Speaking of a discerning man of younger years," Caroline Selby observed in his wake. "Your Sergeant Kingsley knew my husband while in his childhood, did he tell you?" Caroline asked now.

Ursula returned back on guard. "He has."

"He filled my Aaron's last moments with joy. Though I do not understand how."

Careful, but the truth. "Neither do I."

"He expressed some sort of obligation, from years ago. Does Sergeant Kingsley speak of this sister, Mrs. Major?"

Careful, careful. Do not lie. "Of her? To me? No."

"Well. I hope she lives and is well. I would dearly like to tell her how she was the source of the light in my husband's eyes in his final moments. I do not doubt my Aaron's obligation towards the lady. She must be like her brother. Jonathan has been such a help to us over this dreadful time. He is our angel."

"Hmmn. Not a world I would use to describe my sergeant."

"Oh, you do not fool me for a moment. You love each other deeply."

"That does not make him any less irritating."

Chapter Eleven ~ Jonathan

Jonathan loved these drill days. It was like a family reunion, now that Ursula had attached herself to one of the good works organizations. He walked away from all the charities, both religious and secular. On the small rise sheltered by a willow, Miriam was putting out her picnic basket for Sling, his wife, daughters, and in-laws. Jonathan should leave them be, he supposed. His superiors reprimanded him often for fraternizing with the colored families on visiting day. But Sling and his mother were once his family, down in Maryland. And miraculously, here again back before the riots, when they ran Ursula's Gramercy Park home. Then Ursula prevailed upon her Mr. Gardner to give them money to enlarge Sling's farm in Brooklyn. He understood of course. It was only a fraction of what the family owed them for service that spanned generations. But he missed them.

Well, at least his family was being useful. Mr. Gardner and Captain Kane were searching the war-torn South for Sling's missing sisters. Would the Henson family ever be together again? He understood his sister's passion. The Hensons were responsible for the few bright moments of their childhoods. Miriam cast her sheltering arms around them when their mother could not. Sling taught him how to be a good brother, a protector of the women. Jonathan stood powerless while both Ursula and Sling's sisters were sent away. What a cruel way of life plagued the South. It would end. He did not have his sister's wealth and influence, but he would do his part to make it end.

The Hensons left Manhattan soon after the riots and Ursula's childbirth confinement. He missed Miriam's presence in their lives, though she visited often to provide live-out services to Gramercy Park residents and confer with Marie Agathe on running Ursula's household. He understood, of course. So many years Miriam had placed their family above her own. No more. He wondered if Weeksville would ever choose to elect a woman as its mayor. Miriam Henson would be a perfect choice.

Jonathan turned away. He should get back. As he faced the parade ground, he felt a shove at his elbow.

"Wild strawberries showing themselves." Miriam put a slice of pie into his hand. "Eat. You looking ill-fed."

"Not on parade days, with all the delectable donations." He took a bite. The tiny ripe strawberries burst through, rich tender crust. He was transported back to her kitchen and his childhood.

"When this batch of soldiers be sent off?" she brought him back, as they surveyed the emptied parade ground.

"Two weeks."

"Where?"

"It is looking like New Orleans, under Colonel Bliss."

"Far."

"Yes."

"Will they be ready?"

"They are ready now. Rowan tries to keep them here as long as possible. He stretched four weeks to seven this time, under one pretext and another."

"He is a good man. You should not sass him so."

"He does not mind."

She tapped her covered basket at his shin. "I got pies for Miss Ursula and her guests. You up for delivering?"

"Bring it over yourself, Miriam. Ursula will feel hurt if you do not. It will be all right. The charity people are expected to mingle with you all. Only the white officers are not."

She shook her head. "Still getting used to Yankee rules."

"As am I."

"Listen, Master Jon."

He winced. "Now that is a blighted honorific you probably should not use."

"Sergeant Jon," she amended. "I need to tell you something. About one of Miss Ursula's neighbors. Mr. Bell, he hears things."

"What things?"

"From the other chemists."

"In your new home? In Brooklyn?"

"No, not Brooklyn. Around where he used to have the shop, before the riots. Mr. Bell, he still cleaning it out, like all the rest. He be a respected man, Sergeant Jon. Respected by Black and white folk both."

"As are you. Has he asked you yet?"

"Asked what?"

"To marry him, of course."

She frowned but looked down at her small feet. "You in the matchmaking business now?"

"I know the look of the lovelorn in men. Rowan remains sorely afflicted by my sister. My advice to you if Mr. Bell has yet to propose? Stop scaring the man."

"Scaring him? What you talking about?"

"You are a daunting woman, Mrs. Henson. Surrounded by a family who would fight to the death on your behalf. Not just Sling, I'm talking about his wife, in-laws, and children, down to the new baby in his Lena's womb. Poor Mr. Bell must be terrified of the alliance."

"Sergeant Jon, you were born under a silly star."

He shrugged. "Well, you would know."

"If I tell you we got wedding plans and a date, will you let me say my own piece?"

"What date?"

"Sunday, twenty-first day of August. Now will you—"

"How splendid. I shall clear my calendar. Oh, if I am invited to attend."

"'Course you are invited, you crazy man."

"Is Ursula? And all her entourage?"

Miriam frowned, considering. "All but the Booths."

"Booths? The actors? Have you seen how much they eat? Of course not the Booths. I have my standards. They are low, but I have them."

"Good. Because I have hear-tell for you about that young one."

"Edwina?"

"Edwina? Baby Henry's playmate?" She laughed. "Not <u>that</u> young! Youngest playacting Booth, I speak of."

The distasteful brother. "John Wilkes."

"That one. Chemists call him Doctor Booth."

"His latest stage role? In The Devil and Dr. Faustus, perhaps?"

"No. For his orders of quinine. Too much for a bout with the fever. A regiment's worth."

"Regiment?"

"Packed away with his playacting trunks, maybe? To the Southland."

"Smuggled."

"Possible."

"Thank you, Miriam."

"You know I did my best, down in Mary's land. To help the travelers and the sea captains move along the day of Jubilo. But here. It be different."

"Yes. You are free."

"Free? Pish. Spoken like a white man. You think we can walk free and equal among you?"

"No. Of course. Most especially after the riots. I beg your pardon, Miriam. No. Not free." He frowned. "Not even safe."

"It a different kind of hiding than in Mary's land. But the same laying low. Got to keep me, my family and Mr. Bell out of this, you hear? We needs keep Weeksville safe and hidden away from whites who think like the Young Booth."

"How does he think?"

"You know. This country was formed for the white folk, not for the Black, says he in his after dinner talk when his brother's not in ear's space. And Slavery? It be one of the greatest blessings that God ever bestowed upon a favored nation, says he."

"Yes. I understand."

"And you and Captain Buckley, you got to keep your sister safe, too. Your own side, they was out to throw us both under the train tracks. And her with that precious child inside her."

"That was a different bunch, getting hoodwinked by Southern secret operatives and seeking to take their revenge out on my sister after the Southern spy Rose Greenhow eluded their grasp. The Pinkertons have gone back to Chicago. The Army's in charge of the spying now."

"The Army? Well, then. God help you."

****

Jonathan wondered over and over if he had done the right thing. He was about to find out as he was called before the military intelligence officers. They were four in number, dressed in high boots and cavalry uniforms. Their leader stood behind a desk, reading, as the remaining three strode around the room as if impatient to be astride their horses. None had been introduced.

One of the restless spoke. "We have looked into these quinine purchases, Sergeant. Your informant was quite correct, they are excessive. But John Wilkes Booth is often sick with various aliments. He's even now laid up in his brother's house with an infection, safe from any Southern operatives until he dies or recovers."

"And he's an actor," the second officer pointed out as if Jonathan was some rube from the back of beyond who had never attended a theater. "Actors are notoriously thin skinned and sensitive. He is most likely buying it for his fellow thespians. Always traveling, catching themselves in bad air, always sickly."

"Yes, sir." Jonathan had learned to pepper conversations with superiors with "yes, sirs" and "no, sirs" to keep from losing their attention.

A third, barrel-chested officer stepped forward. "I had the pleasure of being in the audience during his portrayal of Richard III a couple of years ago. It was capital! A wild genius, like his father. Did you ever see the father perform, Sergeant?"

"I have not had the pleasure, sir. When J. Wilkes Booth travels south for engagements, he brings trunks—"

"Loaded with an array of costuming, surely. Not secret caches of quinine."

The reading officer at least did not seem interested in the wonders of the theater. When he looked up, he suddenly commanded the attention of the other three. "Yes, excellent work, comprehensive report. Thank you, men," he dismissed them.

They nodded and left the room. Confused, Jonathan turned to follow. "Kindly remain, sir, and take a seat."

Now what?

"Sergeant, you assisted in bringing a slave catcher to justice last year. That this man was your own father."

He was not expecting this pivot. "Hardly justice if the old sinner was exchanged." Too bitter, he reprimanded himself. "Sir."

"Another member of your family, a sister, was a spy suspect who has since disappeared on her way into Canadian exile. You have interesting relatives, sir. You must feel quite outnumbered in your political view."

A mistake. It was a mistake, telling them about Booth, and the quinine. "My sister is innocent, sir."

"She remains married to Captain Buckley, despite his new friendship with a certain philanthropic widow?"

Jonathan resisted the urge to grind his teeth. "We are both her friend. And my sister remains innocent, sir," he maintained, feeling the sweat trickle down his back.

"Is this view held by her husband as well?"

"Yes. Captain Buckley and I have contributed evidence regarding the events in Maryland."

The officer thumbed through pages. "Some time ago, yes."

Too many pages. Jonathan had hoped that Pinkerton and his crew had left without divulging all their findings. And the conclusions they had drawn. He wished he could read the neat Spencerian handwriting better while viewing it upside down.

"Yes," the officer continued, "an account of exploits in the Washington city hospital is well recorded. My. Your captain is quite a sharpshooter."

"My sister's life was hanging on a thread at the moment he killed the prisoner, sir."

"Prisoner of war. Wounded prisoner. Her patient."

"Who had a knife at her throat."

"Yes. Quite. The Catholic Church is embroiled in this business involving Mrs. Buckley, as she was a nursing sister of Charity before her change of mind about leading a celibate life and her somewhat hasty marriage to Captain Buckley. it appears she inherited an estate of undetermined value when she married Captain Buckley. Even our people cannot seem to find out its extent. If she is proved a traitor to the Union, it will all be confiscated, of course. And the Baltimore diocese once thought itself deserving of at least a percentage of her holdings, once she took her vow of poverty. Which she was kept from doing because of the thirty year old age stipulation in her father's will, yet to be achieved. Oh, this is very complicated.

"And then there was a priest who was an imposter, and a nun who has since disappeared. The new archbishop of Baltimore is not pleased about any of this. You were raised according to its precepts, as was your Irish brother-in-law. So I assume you both are aware that the Catholic Church is a powerful institution, Sergeant. One we must tread lightly around."

"Of course, sir."

"You and Captain Buckley have done some good undercover work. The last was performed masquerading as Confederate Zouaves in the midst of our fighting at Gettysburg. Exemplary service, it says here. Why were you placed in your current assignment on Rikers Island?"

"We requested it, sir."

"Requested? No one requests a command training contraband Black men."

"Well, we did, sir."

"I will not ask if proximity to the young widow was among your considerations." A half smile. Of understanding, or bravado? He should be better at reading men. Jonathan wished Rowan or Sling were here. They had a whole lifetime of oppression to build up the skill.

The mysterious commander nodded. Why did Jonathan feel he was about to be shoved off a cliff?

The officer spoke again. "While here, you have nothing but reprimands from your superiors concerning your methods of command. However, your graduates have shown excellent soldiering while on the field of battle. Listen. I wonder if your current training duties might be supplemented now and then."

Another pivot, Jonathan thought. What was he up to now? "Supplemented, sir?" Damn. He was playing that Irish questioning game of Rowan's.

"Yes. It seems you have remarkable Black non-commissioned officers, like Sergeant Henson. Affording you some time, for other duties? I wonder if we may convince you and Captain Buckley to lend your talents to some information gathering here in this city of sedition?"

Good God, Jonathan thought. Spying, again. Rowan is going to have my head. He wondered if he could blame it all on Miriam.

Chapter Twelve ~ Magnus

St. Lawrence Hall, Montreal, Canada
Summer, 1864

Magnus hated Montreal. The LaChine Canal had opened western commerce and made it the largest city in British North America. But it still contained too many of the lazy French, who were more interested in food and dancing than sacred doctrine. For the Quebecois, the sacraments were celebrated, not committed to. And the displays of affection, the laughter. One would never know that the world was exploding just to their south. Except that they welcomed Union soldiers who arranged for weapons shipments from France.

He suppressed a shudder. Never mind his general disgust with this city, Magnus told himself. Concentrate on training these men, these young men, on fire with purpose. And biddable, unlike his son, his stubborn son, who could not be drawn away from his mother, his sister, no matter the lure. No even with a horse, a new saddle. Those steady, accusing eyes. Sometimes his wife's second spawn did not look human at all, but a creature she had created without him.

Back to task. He had seen what this weapon could do. The federals had rained Greek fire on Vicksburg. He'd been caught there after the prisoner exchange. Caught with his latest coffle of slaves, headed for Texas. Stopped by the Greek Fire. It had set the city alight. It had lost him his latest fortune when the Blacks got out of restraints and ran behind Grant's lines in the night.

Greek Fire allowed Grant to cut the Confederacy in two. Well, he would wreak that havoc on New York.

"Stir in more pine resin," he instructed the men.

It was a largely uninhabited portion of Montreal. Lookouts were on duty, should their smoke attract the attention of a workman off the dirt paths, or a night watchman.

"I wish we had more light, Mr. Burwell."

"You have the measuring devices. You should be able to do this in your sleep," he berated them.

"We are not chemists, sir."

They were young, and not interested in correct proportions. More interested in their days of living off the dwindling coffers of the Confederacy.

Patience. It was the gift of his maturity. They must bide their time. Concentrate on the task at hand. Magnus had seen what damage Greek Fire could do. It was an ancient device. In story and song, it had brought the walls of Troy down, struck fear into the hearts of the Crusaders as they tried to take Jerusalem. But the proportions remained secret, undeciphered. He and Phil had worked hard to recreate its elements. He should bring her into this part, to their after dark experiments. She'd strike fear into the hearts of these young pups.

He and Phil, they had been partners for a long time. And she chose loyalty to him, over, even, the church. They would not be thwarted by these impatient young men.

Chapter Thirteen ~ Penina

Penina was in her old bedroom on the house's second floor, though she would not tell the widow that. The pretty peach-colored papers she and her mother had chosen for the walls were still there, but her one bedside bookshelf now had filled companions on three of the walls. They were cabinetry in the gothic style, with cherry wood shelves so high that there was a sliding ladder. Even she could reach the top levels with that ladder. Copies of *Godey's Lady's Book* were strewn about a lower shelf, along with a basket of yarn and a half-finished baby's cap. Instead of the plain wooden floorboards and the oval braided rug of her family's time here, an oilcloth of a geometric design now graced the entire floor. The room had become a library, complete with a central baize cloth covered table. Penina recognized its hand-hewn design from those she'd admired in the window of the shop run by Burns and Trainque.

She placed her traveling pasteboard box on the library table and turned toward the handsome, polished rosewood secretary. After a quick glance at the doorway, Penina slid open a drawer. Yes, the label read that it was crafted by the Meeks brothers. She ran her fingers over its delightful pockets and secret spaces begging to be explored. There was a letter on its surface, alongside a steel pen and inkwell. Penina looked closer. The letter was in the French language. Did Mrs. Major allow her housekeeper to use her library? Would she ever allow Penina to visit this room on her own? Perhaps to borrow from among all these books? How did she even know which ones to choose? Had Mrs. Major read them all?

Penina suppressed the urge to climb that ladder, to learn the titles and stories inside all those books. Her simple pasteboard box looked childish next to the wonder of her bedroom, transformed. Never mind. She lifted its lid and set up her watercolors and brushes on the library table and concentrated on the task at hand.

"Do you enjoy reading, Penina?"

The widow stood at the doorway in the afternoon light streaming through the lace curtained double windows. Looking glorious, despite the askew braiding of hair by her ear that her baby's fingers always entangled as he fell asleep in her arms.

"Well enough. But I have little time for it."

"Oh? But—"

"Neither do you. We must find you a new husband among your admirers, Mrs. Major. So that HRB might have a father."

Mrs. Major looked at her wedding ring. "I have no desire for a new husband."

Penina put down her paintbrush. "Why is that? You are much younger than my mother, and she is baking pies for Sergeant Harrigan."

"Oh? How interesting." Mrs. Major sat between the windows in a tufted chair no doubt constructed by the finest craftsmen and upholsterers of the city. "I am so fond of both Sergeant Harrigan and your mother. Tell me more."

Penina knew that trick. "Oh, no. You are not changing the subject. Look, I have brought a box filled with fans, aired them out and doused them with lilac water so that they do not smell of the fire. None are burnt and the colors I am painting on them will match the items of your new wardrobe."

Mrs. Major frowned. Frowned, as if her recent acquisition of deep blue and lilac half-mourning gowns had been a chore instead of a delight after her year clad in black. The expression did not even make her look ugly, as all the etiquette books promised. The woman was quite impossible.

"Very well then," she finally conceded.

"I knew I could convince you. You will not have your looks forever, you know. My mother has only Sergeant Harrigan, who I was afraid was going to become one of your conquests. Thank goodness he does not try to kiss you on the sly, like Captain Buckley."

"When did you—?"

"Monday last, behind the rain barrel. I am small, as you have observed. I know how to disappear. And this was my home. I have remembered some hiding spots. Papa used to hug Mama there, as she was hanging out the wash." With effort, Penina made the trembling lip that the memory evoked disappear into a wide smile. "You like kissing Captain Buckley, do you not?"

Mrs. Major sighed. "Very much," she admitted.

Why did this woman tolerate such arrogance from her? And how much further could she go, Penina wondered. Would she ever be invited into the widow's bedroom, so she might look for traces of Captain Buckley's intimate presence? What was the look of lovers? Penina blushed as she remembered crouching behind the rain barrel and how her Irish captain pressed his lips all the way down the widow's neck as if she were made of sugar plums.

"But you must try the others too. They would all like to kiss you, I think. Except for Sergeant Kingsley. He has had many opportunities, for you are often alone. I am forced to conclude that he has no interest in becoming your husband. Although he loves to growl and tease you."

Her cheeks flamed. "Sergeant Kingsley is very like a younger brother, and I treasure his company."

"But he is always in disagreement with Captain Buckley. Most disrespectful towards his superior, who could have him shot."

"Penina, my dear friends are not professional soldiers. They are not so mindful of rank when not in circumstances that call for it."

"And they train colored soldiers, without complaint. Mr. Burwell says that is unnatural. He says that white men seal all our doom when they arm the Blacks."

The widow took command of her full attention with those almost golden eyes. "Penina, you have been among our soldiers on Rikers Island. What do you say?"

There was no escape. Her mouth went dry. "I say… why, I say colored folks should be able to fight for the cause."

Mrs. Major smiled. She was almost too beautiful when she smiled. "I agree. Our captain and sergeant feel honored by their duty. It so closely ties with the purpose of this terrible war. These men in their charge are fighting for their own freedom."

"I meant the Union cause, Mrs. Major."

"But our country cannot be made whole while any of its people are enslaved, can it?"

"They will desire citizenship. Even to vote."

"I would like to vote. Would you?"

"No! We have to close the shop, the men get so drunk on Election days."

"Hmmm, yes. That will have to change, would it not, if we all had the vote?"

"Again, you steer me towards serious things to think upon!"

"Do I?"

"It is not a woman's place to dwell too deeply on matters of consequence."

"What a notion. From someone who runs a growing business with her mother," Mrs, Major challenged.

"Under a sign that still reads 'Thomas Selby, Mercantile,' now hanging over my father's old peddling cart. My mother is a widow, like you. I am an orphan, like your baby. But Mama and I are not rich, as you are. What is the source of your estate?"

"My father granted me my inheritance."

"There. We both derive what means we have from dead men."

"Goodness, Penina. You are quite correct." Mrs, Major rose and lifted the lace at her window to view the gardens below them.

"And you have done it again. Made our talk of weighty consequence. Fans, Mrs. Major." Penina drew one from the box. "You must begin practicing your signaling with the Booth brothers, who are your most fashionable suitors, and are surely well-versed in the language of the fan. The signals come from ancient times, with their most recent revival being at the Bourbon court of France."

"I doubt even the Bourbon court was this silly."

"Mrs. Major, you promised."

"I am sorry." She stifled her laughter. "And I am listening." She returned to Penina's worktable.

"Look here. Once I complete my watercolor of forget-me-nots, this one should accompany your charming, if out-of-fashion beribboned blue gown."

Mrs. Major looked over Penina's shoulder at her quick strokes. "How lovely and assured your style is.

But it is not the time for such light colors on me, I think."

"Why? You wish to disappear in half-mourning?"

"Is that not the proper observance?"

"Nonsense. None of the young widows are observing thirty months these days. Unless they were wives of generals. What rank was your man when he went down in battle?"

Her eyes darted about the colors of Penina's paintbox. "Sergeant," Mrs. Major said, just above a whisper. "He was my sergeant."

"You married a sergeant?"

She fixed her eyes on her simple wedding ring now. "N-no. He had advanced to the rank of lieutenant at the time of our wedding."

So, her husband had lasted. Long enough for a raise in rank, and a wedding. Months? A year? It had been enough time to conceive a child. Could only a vigorous man help her to conceive? And so, did her husband give her hope of his recovery? Despite the joy the widow took in the company of her admirers, she had loved him, her fallen husband. Penina could see it now. She was not heartless, or unfeeling. Why had she thought so? Had Mr. Burwell put the thought in her mind?

Penina closed one of her painted fans and tapped the widow's trembling hands lightly. "Leave propriety to the generals' wives with grown children and a third of their husband's estate to look after them. A year is enough. Your baby needs a papa. Sit, please. Now, allow the fan rest on your right cheek, please."

"Like this?"

"Just so."

"And this means…?"

"'Yes.'"

"Ah. Permission."

"Exactly. Holding it to your left cheek signifies 'no.'"

"Could I not merely nod and—"

"Mrs. Major," Penina warned.

"I beg your pardon. Go on."

"Here's one you are sure to need with Captain Buckley…handle to your mouth please."

Ursula obeyed. "And this means…?"

"Kiss me."

Ursula opened the fan and waved it before her flushed cheeks.

"Oh, stop that."

"That?"

"What you are doing, Mrs. Major."

"Is not a fan, meant to be used—"

"I mean how you are moving the fan now: slowly. For then it means 'I am married,' you see."

"Oh, she will need that one," Captain Buckley said from the doorway. My. Her soldiers were visiting her more regularly. Who was minding their troops while they minded the baby now in Captain Buckley's arms?

"Nee-nee" little Henry exclaimed what Penina was becoming convinced was his version of her own name.

Mrs. Major disappeared behind her fan as she dissolved in giggles.

Beside his superior officer, Sergeant Kingsley frowned. "Our little thief makes you laugh almost as much as we and HRB do. I am eaten with envy," he observed tartly.

Captain Buckley lifted the baby higher. "What do you say, Henry? Are we already worthless men being replaced by this slip of a girl, with her hats, fans and gee-gaws?"

The widow let the fan rest on her left cheek then danced it across.

"Mrs. Major," Penina said. "You have just now signaled...why, do you already know the language of the fan?"

"Well, I was a girl once too, dear heart."

"Signaled what?" the bigger man asked.

"Now, that is our secret, Captain," the widow told him before taking Henry from his arms. "Oh, you smell so sweet, my darling," she cooed. "And are quite dry."

"Of course he is," Sergeant Kingsley said.

"We are not completely useless," his captain affirmed.

They had changed Baby Henry's diapers? Mrs. Major's soldiers were the most peculiar men she had ever met, Penina decided.

Chapter Fourteen ~ Magnus

July 16, 1864

Magnus Kingsley sat and waited on the bluestone steps. He'd left his keys with Caroline Selby, along with his rooms' belongings, signs of trust. It was to keep paying his false court of the woman and her daughter. A distasteful pair, who reminded him too much of, well, never mind.

That damned man of theirs had refused to succumb to his injuries. So Phil helped him hatch a plan. A nice, gradual plan, until he realized their mark was not the merchant Thomas Selby at all, but Shulmann the peddler. And he was no longer at death's door. He might come home to recognize the boarder his wife had taken in, despite Magnus' full beard, and the years between their last confrontation. Who did the peddler think he was, arguing against a father's right to lay his strap on his own son? It still made him angry, over a dozen years later.

Yes, Shulmann would have suspected his identity at least, because he was a sharp-eyed Jew. So, Phil took on the job of hospital cook, and made her apple crisp, fed to the recovering husband and his hovering policeman friend both. Phil was nothing if not thorough. But the dosage was off. One did its work, the other did not. Harrigan survived, and policemen were notoriously suspicious. And this one was also a widow hunter. So he and Phil had to disappear for awhile. He'd left her in Montreal, trying out more recipes for Greek Fire with the men. He had returned, to make sure there were no inquiries at the hospital, then send for her.

As for him, he hoped that absence would make his widowed landlady's heart grow fonder. He straightened his new brocade vest, French made, bought by way of the Confederate commissioner in Canada.

For now, he would keep up his courting of the Jew storekeeper's women. Magnus knew that he was losing his once towering strength. And he no longer turned all female heads with a look and a smile. But he was a better widow hunter now.

He had thought the two more wealthy. Did they not live in a fine house and a fashionable neighborhood? They were probably hoarding the Jew's money. Easy prey, especially if he turned the silly daughter of that bright-eyed woman completely over to his side, and against the Gramercy Park war widow, under her black veils and discrete wanderings. Because he wanted to know more of her, he realized now, although she was likely a Republican, and he could not pretend to be an "all for the Union" man. She hid how rich she was, even from him, who had eyes and ears all over the city of New York. Such wealth meant allies, strong ones. His specialty was preying on the weak. But damn all the warnings. He was an experienced operative. He was Colonel Burwell! He wanted his chance at her, and her fortune. So, when he learned that she lived in the Jew's former home, what was easier than turning the young one against her, the usurper of the silly girl's precious garden?

Magnus stood and climbed the small landing in front of the house they shared and looked over the street. Where were they?

There, approaching, arms laden with baskets of colorful flowers and summer fruit. They looked different, somehow. Not as stricken with worry, not as needy. That might prove to be a problem.

"Mr. Burwell. You are returned from your latest sojourn."

He removed his hat, displaying his fine head of silver, leonine hair. "I am, dear lady. Do I find you well?"

"Quite well, sir. Penina and I are bringing in berries to boil into a compote that may prove healthful to you after your journey."

He turned to the brat. "Has Mrs. Major allowed you some of the fruits of your own planting efforts, then, Miss Selby?"

"Oh, you must not frown so when you speak of Mrs. Major, sir," the child said, practicing her coquetry in a way that set his teeth on edge. "Not any more. We have become good companions since you went away."

"Is that so?"

"She is opening up new opportunities for Mama and me among her friends. We are fashioning hats and fans for their pleasure. And once Mrs. Major spoke to our common landlord, we have our own fruits to bring forth. Mama thinks our new friend convinced him to make it so, imagine! And Mrs. Major is very beautiful, with so many admirers—soldiers and actors and artists and a sea captain. Why, I have had to advise her on the language of flowers and the fan both to keep them all in line. And she has the most delightful baby, all round, laughing and—"

"Please bring these baskets inside, Penina," her mother put a merciful end to the child's babble. "Poor Mr. Burwell looks weary and has no interest in hearing of Mrs. Major."

Magnus had forgotten how young girls could be charmed by babies. "Oh, but you are mistaken, dear ladies. I am most interested in this woman whose mention has helped bring the bloom back to your cheeks," he insisted.

Chapter Fifteen ~ Jonathan

The Old Grapevine was full of its usual inhabitants: Actors and artists celebrating their latest successes and patronage, politicians and charlatans. How Jonathan wished they allowed women in here. Ursula would separate the spies from patriots from the harmless blowhards with one swish of one of Penina's colorful fans, one knowing look into their heart of hearts. He placed the fancifully painted salesman's box he'd borrowed from Mrs. Selby at his feet. It contained her daughter's discarded items—projects to improve hair ornaments and fans that did not please her. The wretched little garden thief had driven a hard bargain with him, even for them.

"No hawking of any wares in here," the aproned man behind the bar warned.

"I seek only a watering hole after a long day trodding uptown establishments, my good man," Jonathan tried to assure him.

"Even so, I am watching you, Marylander."

So much for laying low. This spying business was complicated. But at least his Eastern Shore accent was still intact, after so much exposure to nasal-toned Yankees. Jonathan sat back in the loose-jointed Windsor chair whose paint had long since worn off and listened. Perhaps if he reported the conversations to Ursula, she would help him sort it all out. He concentrated on three men, whose diction and flaring nostrils betrayed them as tragedians.

"What if the Peace Democrats do not prevail in the November elections? What if Lincoln wins?"

"He will not win. He has called for another five hundred thousand men. From where will they come after the short work this city made of his draft efforts last summer?"

"We are all tired of this war. Only abolitionists, preachers, profiteering contractors and the political press want this carnage continued. How many recruits will come out of them?"

Jonathan tried entering the conversation quietly. "If Lee can hold Richmond and Johnson overcomes Sherman's forces in Georgia, Lincoln may be defeated on the field and in the election."

Three tragedian heads went up, turned to scrutinize his worn peddler clothes. Only one smiled. "True.

All that's needed is the Confederacy's unflinching nerve. Have we seen you in here before?"

"I have not had the pleasure of visiting this establishment before now. I am visiting my sister and her brood over in Gramercy Park. Tonight I am in need of more manly company." True enough. Though Jonathan would have preferred Adam Badeau's more aesthetically interesting circles.

"Travel to our city often?"

"As I deal in preposterous trifles from fans to silk flowers, all aimed at the newly thriving wives of cursed war profiteers, yes."

He hoped they would not demand a look into his box. The contents would hardly pass muster among the house servants of war profiteers.

But a greying tragedian took hold of his shoulder, not the paste and cardboard box. "Be advised to keep watch, young tradesman," he said in a perfect diction stage whisper. "The officers of our occupying Army frequent these rooms after," he consulted his watch, "nine o'clock. From then until closing time, it is better to listen than to express our views, even here in what is still Fernando Wood's city."

"As listening is my specialty, I am in the right place." Jonathan took some personal pride in being a truth-telling spy, when possible.

"And who sent you here?"

"An associate who values information."

"Hmm. You bear the talk style of some of our fellow traveling companions."

"Perhaps Doctor B.?" a younger actor prompted. "You feeling as poorly with the yellow fever, friend?"

There. The smuggled quinine link to Booth that Miriam had given him, established by a fellow thespian. Miriam said the chemists had taken to calling him Dr. Booth for the copious amounts of the drug he purchased. As much as he liked Edwin, he'd like to get the pompous J. Wilkes Booth out of his sister's social circle and into the federal prison at Fort Lafayette.

"If so, I would be at the Five Points chemist for my supply of powders, would I not?"

Was that good enough? Knowledge of the chemist's location?

Jonathan was under the older, portly one's scrutiny now. "You keep us guessing, friend."

The other tried to be helpful. "Maybe he's part of the younger crew that Colonel B., not Doctor B. gathers about him when in the Emerald City?"

Do all Southern spies go by B? Jonathan had no idea the contact person he would name if pressed. And he would surely be pressed. They were looking for a signal, not riddles answering their own. He was glad when, at that moment, Rowan, his borrowed sergeant's uniform opened and displaying a stained blue vest, came barreling through the doors. He was supported by Sergeants Hayes and MacNeel who had demoted themselves to privates, on each arm.

"A round for the house, barkeep!" Rowan shouted, his Irish accent and cadence exaggerated, "I am about to send another regiment of Black devils into the maw of Lee's forces!"

A less than hearty cheer and a few raised glasses were all the thanks he got from the beneficiaries of his largess. The actors left Jonathan's side to have their glasses filled. But a few patrons moved closer to his brother-in-law, displaying their interest. Jonathan got a good look, committing their faces to memory.

Except for the incident with his long-ago gift of peach brandy that he hoped would facilitate some sparks between his sister and this man, Jonathan had never known Rowan to imbibe anything stronger than a glass or two of hard apple cider that Marie Agathe poured for him. How was he now acting such a convincing drunkard? Perhaps he should take to the stage like the Booths. Did they ever frequent this place? He had met and conversed with Wilkes, who knew that Jonathan was no civilian salesman. The

Booths knew Rowan too, and his correct captain's rank. Jonathan stepped toward his brother-in-law.

"What a sorry duty you have, my friend."

"Aye, sir. But have not a concern. The rebels will cut them down right quick. Still, I would much rather be sending the imps of Lucifer back to Africa myself."

"Sergeant, this is unseemly," Hayes and MacNeel said, rather woodenly, Jon thought. They probably had not participated in even amateur theatricals back in their Maine hometown.

Rowan slapped their backs. "Men, do not have fear on my behalf. I have learned that the Grapevine here is a haven for the free speech guaranteed us."

"Free? That might have been, before the war," one of Jonathan's interested faces commented. "Before restricted speech, the press, and the suspended writ of Habeas Corpus."

"Aye, before they put that ape in charge." said the other.

MacNeel's face flushed with anger, and a vein appeared at Hayes' temple. No, they likely did not even practice dramatic recitations in their youth. Time for them to go. Jonathan stepped closer to the trio.

"Worry not about your Sergeant! He is safe here with us. But the two of you strapping fellows— you should be in the arms of more tender company. Might

I interest you in Parisian painted fans for luring a sweetheart or two? Not only fans, mind you, but a card to decipher the secret coded language by which women communicate to you and each other of their feelings and pliability. Worth its weight in gold dust this information is, but for you?" He looked up to see an expected furious reaction from the barkeep. "Well, shall we continue our business outside, as our benevolent proprietor rightly does not want the sale of any but his goods within these lofty walls?" He continued leading them out the doors.

Finally, some use of that flibbertigibbet girl and her wares, Jonathan thought when they were finally among the leaves of the ancient grapevine rising up the side of the tavern's massive chimney. He wondered if it had listened to General Washington's spies during the revolution.

The men protested leaving officers without their armed guards.

"Never mind that. Take off your hats."

"Our hats? Why?"

"Sign of respect, of course."

They did, without objection.

"Now, give me a dollar."

"What for?"

"The fans."

"But they're not worth more than—"

"What women-starved soldiers think they are worth! Come on, boys, make me out to be a convincing salesman. Assume we are being watched and give me a dollar."

"Yes, sir."

"Each."

"Each?"

"Now, that reaction was most convincing, Hayes. Good work. Now, go."

"But—"

"Where, sir?" MacNeel asked.

Jonathan sighed. "The docks. Mingle there, ears open, for an hour. Then walk further north, engage a ferry boatman and return to camp. Tell our commanding officer that Captain Buckley and I will be back by first light, if I can get him out of his lover's bed."

The tops of their ears turned red. Why did he enjoy scandalizing them so much? Well, no time to stop. "Better tell him noon, she is a very beautiful woman. And give those fans to a couple of trollops. That is an order."

"Yes, sir," Hayes said, almost standing at attention.

But his fellow sergeant shook Jonathan's hand, seeing through all his nonsense. "Have a care, sir."

"We will. Thank you, MacNeel." Jonathan smiled. "And, worry not, Captain Buckley and I will make good liars out of you yet."

When he returned inside the Old Grapevine, Jonathan found Rowan the center of attention of a corner of the room, along with the men who had shown their initial interest. The three actors were not among them. Where had they gone? He had yet to acquire knowledge of their names. Well, to the task at hand, how to invade that corner?

"Ah, my deliverer!" Rowan solved the problem for him. "Come join us, friend." he urged, while signaling the proprietor of the bar for another round of drinks. "Mr. Abbot here is expressing his views of our glorious future."

His brother-in-law was not half the drunken fool as was on display to his new friends. He had gotten the name of one of their targets. And Jonathan surmised only he could see the relief behind his kinsman's easy smile. He was a handsome man, despite the off-kilter look the scarring and glass eye gave his face. Jonathan understood why his sister had fallen for her Irishman so hard, so fast.

Once the barman had filled his glass, Rowan took a quick sidelong glance at a nearby spittoon. Jonathan suspected most of his bourbon was landing there. And on that already soaked vest.

Rowan belched extravagantly. Even that was more amusing than disgusting. "Pray continue, Mr. Abbot, of whichever Carolina you say you are from."

Abbot, a tall man of middle years with a neatly trimmed beard, frowned, but continued to hold court among his admirers. "It is not the Carolinas, or any state in the Confederacy of which I speak. I speak of this city, this ground on which we tread."

"…And do business," Jonathan contributed, tucking his wares box more neatly under his arm.

"Indeed," Abbot approved. "Imagine, gentlemen. Once we take back New Orleans, New York will join her. The free city of New York would shed light and hope of a future reconstruction of our blessed confederacy. The grains from the country's midlands, the minerals from the west— all our wealth travels over the veins of our waterways, to these ports and out into the world."

"And how do we make New York this free city?"

"We take it back from these war profiteers with their mansions going up Fifth Avenue."

"Aye, those bastards!" Rowan exploded suddenly. "Hiring the Irish at slave wages— our lads to drive their carriages in all weathers, dig their holes in the ground and rail beds. And our lasses. Aye, our lasses shedding the bloom of youth, for what? To clean their bedpans."

Abbot's shorter, companion raised a righteous finger in Rowan's face. "Exactly so. Do not forget the profiteers and their lazy sons stealing the maidenheads of your sisters."

"It turns my thoughts black, Mr. Cantwell." Rowan formed his fingers into a fist. Jonathan hoped it would not crush the man's nose.

Another name. Abbot and Cantwell. He had identified two.

Abbot came between them. "Consider well. What are you doing, Irishman? Why, you are training Black brutes that are better fit for digging out foundations for those Fifth Avenue mansions. Even the best of them should be cooking and cleaning and waiting on us. Those sooty devils are not for soldiering, not for deadly rifles in their hands. But armed they are, as they work towards victory for the abolitionists. Radical abolitionists. Amalgamators! After a Republican victory, mark my words, the Blacks will be on to full citizenship. Yes, to the vote, and office holding. Soon after? They will be seducing, not just the dock scum, but respectable white women. They will be putting one of their mongrel children in the President's house itself!"

Jonathan watched his brother-in-law rendered speechless.

"What's caught your Irish tongue?" Cantwell prompted, with his own contempt seeping through, Jonathan thought. What was it like to be used to this? He would never be able to survive in his brother-in-law's skin.

"I am a sworn soldier of the Union Army. But what can I do to keep these fearful things from happening, sir?" Rowan asked. Quietly.

"You have more power against this disastrous future than you think. You are training contrabands to kill their owners just as sure as Mad John Brown did. What if they were returned below the Mason and Dixon line for a different task? To work towards Southern victory?"

"Returned? As in the days of the Fugitive Slave Laws?"

"Laws still on the books, that the war and that damned ape in the president's house stopped enforcing."

"Illegally!" Abbot reminded all in their corner.

"You are dreaming, surely." Rowan said in a good projection of his own genuine country mouse wide-eyed wonder. "How can such a thing come to be?"

"With the help of the waterways. Our iron-clad and fish torpedo boats. Once we make New York a free port city. With the help of slave catchers, blockade runners and brave privateer captains. And men of conviction inside the federal Army, who wear union blue only on the outside. Sons of liberty such as yourself, my friend, would be welcome among the Confederate Army of Manhattan."

Rowan shook his head. "Dearly wished, but impossible."

"All at once, perhaps. But a few at a time? Worry not for your own complicity, Sergeant. The negroes that you help us to make disappear? They will be thought deserters. Or presumed drowned. The sea is so convenient toward our purpose."

"Even so, I will get some of the blame. My damned Yankee Protestant commanders hate us, who have earned our extra stripes whipping these Blacks into soldiers. Maybe I will be sent to an even worse position— like guarding those miserable rebel prisoners of war in their holding places."

"Just so!" Cantwell enthused, before he got a quieting look from Abbot, who spoke in a soothing tone.

"If there, we would not abandon you, my friend. And we would have great, noble use for you."

Once back at Ursula's house, Rowan hung up the matted and stained sergeant's coat in the closet beside the kitchen hearth. "Puts me in mind of the priest holes in Ireland." he said softly.

Jonathan hoped his brother-in-law spoke about his life in Ireland to Ursula, for in moments like this, it seemed to weigh upon him worse than the war weighed upon them both. She could help him. She could help him carry that burden.

But Jonathan understood knowledge of their shared Catholic history, at least. "Hiding priests brought a lot of soul-redeeming sacraments to many of our ne'er do well ancestors in centuries past, eh, brother?" he tried.

A weary smile from the man. Success.

Jonathan turned to find the small, formidable woman who had raised Ursula and himself standing, fists tense at her side. Damnation. Did the woman never sleep?

"What are you two about now?" Miriam demanded.

"No good," Rowan confessed.

"I did not know you were visiting, Miriam," Jonathan tried. "My, life in the wiles of Brooklyn agrees with you, you have never looked more lovely. Or is it the effect of Mr. Bell's attentions?"

"Whist!" she silenced him fiercely, before peering into the closet storage space. Her nose wrinkled in displeasure. "Master Jon's fancy man's patched silk coat be next to yours in there, Captain Buckley. You both working for Pinkerton again?"

"Pinkerton's back in Chicago," Rowan answered. "Army is running its own spy service now, Miriam."

"Lord help us. They still looking for her?" She cocked her head toward the stairway.

"Yes," Jonathan tried to enter her good graces again. "We were trying to find out about that, through the information on the quinine smuggling you gave me, when—"

Miriam's frown deepened. "When you got your-selfs recruited into their dirty, dissembling business again instead," she finished for him, shaking her head.

"What is this business?" Marie Agathe asked, be-wildered, as she stood in the doorway, a pail of Henry's diapers in her hand.

"Spy work," Miriam said.

"Oh. Oh, bien. Much better. Your poor wife, Rowan, she thinks you are at the bordellos deep into the night. You must tell her you are finding the seditionists only."

"But that's the nature of it," Rowan tried to explain to them both. "Keeping the two lives separate."

Marie Agathe folded her arms. "Not in this house. There will be no separate. Rien du tout! Now take off those whiskey pantaloons and go make some love with your broken in the heart wife."

Once Rowan tromped up the stairs, Jonathan found himself at the mercy of the two women.

"I worry about that one," Miriam reprimanded him. "He knows not how to dissemble."

Her counterpart patted her shoulder. "He is of the Irish, mon amie. He got his own bag full of dissembling. The English, they make it necessary for us Quebecois and the Irish both, eh?"

"What are you grinning at?" Miriam demanded of Jonathan, who thought he had disappeared from their attention. "Got no such worries on your account. You plenty good at this."

He broke off a piece of her corn cake. "I learned from the best, 'Yes Master, No, Master, I got no brains for such like thinking Master,'" he said, ready to avert the snap of her dish towel.

Instead, she only widened her eyes in amusement before she pulled him aside. "Bureau of Colored Troops being any better about this latest batch of enlisted?"

He frowned. "No. 'More order and structure!' Also: 'the 'regular' Army fights to save the Union, not to free negroes.'"

"Huh. These 'not regular ones' willing to fight just fine at Fort Wagner, Big Cabin, Honey Springs."

He nodded. "They face more danger, Miriam. The Confederate Congress has decreed that if captured they will be executed immediately for servile insurrection, along with their white officers. Still, they train with the utmost dedication. And, you are quite correct, they fight like wildcats."

"Do not you take on that burden of their danger. It is evil not of your making. These men in your charge. They will stir up the winds of change, Sergeant Jon. Even with them fighting two wars at a time." She took his hand, chasing every glib thought from his head. "Thank you for treating them like men, and their women and children, like family."

"They are family, Miriam. You taught me that. I am not the complete idiot I sometimes appear."

"I know that, young one."

"A rapidly aging young one, dear lady."

Chapter Sixteen ~ Ursula

How foolish she was to think she was losing her husband to a fancy woman.

But there were no word games, no endless Irish questioning, and no chastisement of her foolishness tonight. He stood at the wash basin, sponging off the spilled whiskey, the cigar smoke, until he was her Rowan again. Then he spoke softly of his new duties, promising that he and Jon would look out for each other in this city of sedition. That all was worth it for the time spent here, like this, with her. Because time was the only gift he could give her.

Almost without noise he moved, washed, spoke, because the baby was sleeping in the nursery beyond the open doorway close by.

Ursula knew that both sides killed spies outright. A wrong word or move could wipe the two men she loved best from this world. That was all she thought of, at first. It made her mute, it paralyzed her. Until he knelt by the side of the bed, as if he were a supplicant, and she a saint. His kisses began traveling up her arm. She sensed his desperation, his suffering, compounded by her own.

"Come to bed," she whispered.

He did. They stayed in their haven of here, now. What had she ever done to deserve this man? Her heart swelled as she caught glimpses of his glistening fresh-washed black hair, teasing that place between her breasts. She wound her fingers through it, breathed hard and fast as his tongue stroked her breasts. It was easy to imagine them alone in all the world, when they were like this, in the confines of her bed, working with quiet gasps towards each other's delight.

Before morning's light she heard him singing from the nursery, a call and response with the baby's coos, his attempts at words. Rowan stood in the open doorway, dressed again. As a soldier, not a spy, not her lover, her husband, safe in her arms. Their son patted his cheek, keeping good time as he finished the song.

Over the mountains, over the sea

back where my heart is longing to be

Oh, let the lark that sings to me

sing to the ones I love.

He put Henry into bed beside her. "Baby's hungry," he whispered, kissing her brow.

And then he was gone.

Miriam knew her too well. "You got your garibaldi shirtwaist and Zouave jacket on. You going to war with your lawyer?" she demanded as the ferry to Brooklyn approached the dock.

How Ursula missed having Miriam as her daily scheming partner. "Well, two can play at this game of Mr. Gardner's," she said, outlining her plan.

"Lord help the man if he stands in the way of your set mind. Me, I will head home to teach some wedding tart making to Ada and Kali. They are good at the cooking already, like their mama. See you next week, bright and early, child. Big to-do it is turning out to be. Such foolishness!"

"Marrying your wonderful Mr. Bell, foolish? I think not."

"I hope my wonder man don't take flight when he sees all this fuss."

"If so, my men will haul him to the preacher, fear not."

"Go, then, get on with your buying up your island."

"Stay safe on yours, my dear one."

As Ursula entered his office at the appointed time, Mr. Gardner had a report ready and came directly to it.

"You were quite correct to surmise there is trouble around the burnt-out building that housed Selby's Mercantile. The area is in dispute. The building has been condemned. It will come down. The liveryman next door is eying the lot and looks to expand room for his horses. But he thinks the owner should pay for demolition."

"I shall pay for it."

"Why would you do that?"

"To be a good neighbor."

"Neighbor?"

"Yes. You wish me to take a greater interest in my holdings, do you not, Mr. Gardner? It is in a fine section of the street, with poplars planted twenty years ago providing welcome green and shade. And a flower seller maintains a lovely shop on the corner. The smell of his chrysanthemums wafts down the entire block. It is delightful, and should temper the livery's smells, which I do not believe are all that unpleasant, do you? In short: I wish you to offer the price necessary for the property, on its double lot."

"And what if that is too high?"

"Now, Mr. Gardner. It is you who has schooled me that everything has a price. I will leave it to you to find an agreeable one. When it is in possession, offer half the cleared lot to the liveryman, as a gesture of our goodwill. The Selbys have now salvaged what remains of their establishment's goods after the riots. We shall have built a smaller, completely brick structure, to minimize future fire risk."

Her solicitor looked dumbfounded. "We?" he managed to ask.

"You and I, Mr. Gardner. Have we not always worked in tandem?" She arched her brow. "Even without giving me notice of shifting funds and properties?"

Oh dear, that was expressed more pointedly than she would have liked. Was she picking up unladylike habits from these bold New Yorkers? Ursula drew in a calming breath as she reached across the wide table for her solicitor's hand. "This is because we trust each other," she tried to assure him. "I thank you for providing Caroline and Penina their new garden."

"It is your garden," he growled out. "As this new structure will be yours. Have you thought about what it is to become?"

"A millinery. Is that not what they call the places that sell ladies' hats?"

"Ursula, you wish to invest in a business, and you are unsure of what it is called?"

"Oh, not me, Mr. Gardner. It is you who are so fond of Penina's hats, fans, hair ornaments and parasols that you will only rent our establishment to her and her mother."

"No one on earth will believe that."

"Hmmm," Ursula reconsidered. "Another idea, then. You have heard about the Selby women's a la mode sense of fashion from the female members of the illustrious Booth family. They would, of course, insist that all their friends frequent such an establishment, only were it presided over by the mother and daughter wonders of French fashion sense. And so, you have deemed it a wise investment. How does that sound?"

"As mad as the Booths themselves."

Ursula's smile disappeared. "Edwin has expressed fears based on his intimate knowledge of his late father's behavior. His fears are amplified by "common knowledge" tale telling among those who also delight in performances. But I will tell you what I imparted to him: I have detected no sign of infirmness of the mind in any living member of that family, sir. Kindly do not add your voice to those rumors in my presence."

"I merely repeat—"

"As both my mother and I have been accused of such infirmities in order to secure control over our estates, I remain especially sensitive to such rumor mongering about my friends."

"I beg your pardon, Ursula."

"You are forgiven, of course."

Mr. Gardner knew how to achieve forgiveness, she made note. By calling her by her given name. By acting as her friend as well as counselor.

Ursula could not wait to see Caroline and show her the plans. "Look at these drawings, my friend."

"What are these notations?"

"Oh, that is Penina's doing. She would like larger windows in front. She explained her ideas of a larger display opportunity on the street-facing windows."

"Penina did that?"

"Yes. Was it not resourceful of her?"

"Mr. Gardner will surely withdraw his offer and send us on our way."

"Nonsense. Well, I did hear what might have been his teeth grinding. But then he made one of his remarks about his ignorance of such things and promised to bring the matter up with the builder."

"Ursula, what was your part in all this?"

"My part? Beyond singing your praises far and wide?"

"Exactly." The widow's hand was on her arm. There was no escape. "Please do not misunderstand me. Mr. Gardner has always been a good and fair man. But since you came into our lives, he has become a benefactor. You are the connection. And I question his talk of his investors only wishing to take advantage of good business opportunities. Who thinks to invest in poor widows and orphans and their schemes?"

"Who?"

"I understand that he, personally, looks after the holdings of but one investor."

"Do you?"

"And who might that investor be?"

"I cannot imagine." That was the truth, because she already knew. Had Caroline found her out? Would it change the nature of their friendship? Her friend's face was still expectant. Well, Ursula thought, I am not married to an Irishman without learning some of his tricks. She was down to but one question, the one by which she would be found out.

"Who?" she whispered.

"Why, Mr. Gardner himself, Ursula."

"Mr. Gardner?" she whispered.

"Have you never thought the same thing your-self?"

Relief flooded her. "I must confess, I have not." The truth. And she could put a stop to Rowan's infernal question responses to the poor woman who, thankfully, remained ignorant.

Chapter Seventeen ~ Ursula

Weeksville, Brooklyn
August 21, 1864

Miriam had said yes to her shy chemist at last. How Ursula loved weddings. This one was a grand occasion breakfast on the Henson farm in Brooklyn. Sling, resplendent in his sergeant's dress uniform and white gloves, had given his mother away. The brief ceremony was beautiful, officiated by the Union chaplain of her men's Rikers Island training ground, his preacher voice rolling in beautiful, modulated cadences. Jonathan, under Rowan's watchful eye, made sure all the paperwork was duly noted and placed in the Army's care. Mr. Bell was a free man, but Miriam was contraband of a border slave state, making her name part of the Army's records as her freedom was not yet secure.

But there was no sign of fear of slave catchers here in Weeksville. It was another world, where the habitual, protective tension had disappeared from people's faces, leaving only beauty. Bustling shopkeepers, coopers, blacksmiths, bakers attended in their best dresses and suits of clothes. They were neighbors, who had welcomed Miriam and her family, helped them construct their house and barn and storage sheds. Miriam's family had in turn joined them in providing for refugees made homeless by the riots. Manhattan was poorer for their loss. But this thriving neighborhood of east Brooklyn was all the richer.

Joy-filled participants made way for a day of eating, toasting, singing, dancing and games in the meadow that the horses and sheep had graciously cropped into a green carpet for the guests.

Her family and the Selbys, along with a few invited Army officers like Adam Badeau were the only white faces in the sea of celebrants. Ursula felt privileged to be here, in this world that pointed towards possibility. For all the free men and women and children. After the war.

Ursula was glad she and Penina had worked together on the flowered embroidery of Miriam's apron, because the bride was so busy setting the tablecloths to rights in the breeze that she had forgotten to take it off for the ceremony. Still, she was beautiful, her dark hair streaked with shining grey adorned by a lace cap and a few late summer white roses that Penina had carefully made smooth of thorns. The be-spectacled chemist had the scent of lavender in his lapel added to his usual cloves. He also exhibited considerable tolerance of the antics of Miriam's children and grand-children as they pelted the couple with rice and shoes.

Her friend pulled off her apron at last as Ursula dusted the errant rice from her hair. They were both laughing until Miriam took her hand.

"Miss Ursula. You have made all this possible. And something more."

"Oh, not at all."

She frowned. "You forget how far I go back in your life: the morning your mama trusted you into my arms."

"I will grant only that we have been looking out for each other," Ursula claimed. "And that only in our re-cent years together."

"Hmmm." Miriam's mouth formed a hard line. "You are messing with my speechifying, child."

"Oh. I beg your pardon." Ursula made a slight pause, smiling. "Pray continue, Mrs. Bell."

They both grinned at her formality.

Sling stood in the kitchen doorway. "Mama," he called. "They won't stay put. And Captain Kane is eating all the wedding tarts before we can put them out."

"All right then!" A familiar sound of displeasure burst from Miriam's throat. "Those two had me outnumbered since the day they started rumbling their long limbs around inside of me."

"Two?"

"My surprise for you, Ursula. They won't be hidden in the back rooms and away from your sight no more this day. Captain Kane?"

Her father's dearest friend and shipmate stepped out of the scullery, wiping the sweet crumbs from his white whiskers.

"Do you recognize these ladies, Ursula?" he asked quietly, opening the door wider behind him.

She stared hard, even as the women were staring the same way at her.

Miriam's twin daughters, tall and powerful and bright-eyed, shyly covering wide smiles with their work-hardened hands. Yes, she was sure of it, from one's dimpled chin to the other's graceful hold of the other's hand. The same way their brother Sling took hold of his children Ada and Kali. But these two sisters were a head taller than the sea captain.

"Dibb? Nima?"

"It be us all right, Miss Ursula."

"Oh, Captain." She raised shining eyes to Lucius Kane. "You have found them."

"Oh, no. I was not nearly clever enough, though it was not for want of their mother's behest to try, dear heart. None other than Moses herself found them, along with eight hundred others after the raid up the Combahee River in South Carolina."

"Moses? You mean Mrs. Tubman?"

"Oh, it was grand night, Miss Ursula," Dibb proclaimed. stepping forward. "Should have seen our Moses, half the size of a pea pod herself, commanding troops, Black and white alike! Me and Nima, we took up our hoes and joined her right then."

Nima took up her sister's story, just as Ursula remembered from their childhoods together. "We went and marched with her for awhile."

"Least we could do. After the fighting, we stayed close, providing for the troops, doing some nursing work, like she does. My, she is a fierce-some woman, surely sent by God himself."

"Me and Nima, we made off with a set of silver candlesticks and two Argand lamps from the place we worked and kept fed for years. Come good weather, we swapped them for a sail up the coastline to Mary's

Land, in a Yankee clipper almost as fine as Captain Kane's."

Nima frowned. "Dibb never was the best at bartering. But they served us some fine meals of corn cakes and chowder whilst aboard. Imagine…"

"Us being served, after all them years of serving, Miss Ursula."

"Why, we thought it was on account of our Moses had finished off the whole war for Father Abraham!"

Dibb took up their story. "Learned Fenwick Pines was full of Yankees, and they hired what they call 'the likes of us' for real federal money wages. So we went to find Mama and some work there."

"But most everyone we knew was gone from Fenwick."

"Now that French lady Madame Picard who you put in charge of things, Miss Ursula? She treated us fine."

Ursula smiled. "She is Marie Madeline, one of my husband's three, well, I suppose they are his sister godmothers." she told them. "Another sister is Marie Agathe, who runs my household here, and loves our little Henry with all her heart."

"You make powerful alliances, Miss Ursula," Dibb proclaimed.

"And, down in your Mary's Land place, Madame Picard runs the place good and proper like Mama would..." Nima began.

"So that the Yankee soldiers, they can train and nurse themselves after battle time.." her sister continued. "Madame said we'd best stay while we waited for Captain Kane. She gave us a room of our own with a featherbed and only fishing duties for the household."

The smiling captain folded his arms. "And so you see I provided only the last link of the journey. These intrepid women found their own way back to their mother."

Dibb snorted. "No surprise where Mama was. Figured she get to Sling in New York first chance she had."

"That chance was you, hiring her on as a lady's maid and housekeeper in the biggest, grandest city in America."

Ursula stole a look at their mother, her lifelong friend. "Well, I would be foolish not to."

"Didn't figure she'd be running a farm that belonged to her own self."

"To all of you," Ursula said quietly.

"Oh yes, our brother wrote down our new fancy family name. We all Hensons, that right?"

"Quite right!" Ursula laughed. "Except your mother is a fancy married lady now, with her husband's name attached to hers. Oh, I am glad beyond measure to be in your company."

Ursula held out her arms, hungry for the touch of her childhood companions. They obliged and she felt the strength of their years and hard-won freedom in their large, calloused hands. And yet their eyes were kind, their touch gentle. They sat together as Captain Kane slipped back into the heart of the festivities.

No wonder Miriam was distracted at her own wedding. No wonder there was a secret joy trying to hide behind those eyes. Her twins, the gangling girls who taught Ursula how to jump rope and catch fire-flies, were now wide-smiling women, beautiful in their strength, and still finishing each other's sentences.

"So many changes. Master Jon, a soldier? Now that's a wonder. 'Course we always loved him, even when he was a trick riding horse scamp giving your mama the vapors."

"We like your man. And your little child, Miss."

"Rascal, loving the mud, see that, Dibb?"

Nima shook her head. "Like his mama."

Ursula smiled. "And what of your lives? Do you have husbands? Children?"

"Oh, no, Dibb confided. "Not us. At the place we were sent off to, in the Carolinas? The masters were more lazy and lame-brained than usual for no-account white folks. We got good at wrapping ourselves away from the masters with hoo-doo curses."

"Doubled up powerful, on account of we twins," Nima said.

Her sister grinned. "And could poison their supper."

They all went silent as they watched the children play. "We glad Sling found his good woman. But we not made for the menfolk, Miss Ursula," Dibb said with quiet assurance. "We auntie women."

"Like your brother, Master Jon," her sister explained further. "He a uncle man, yes?"

Jonathan, there at the punch bowl, with little Henry pulling on his dress uniform's buttons, casually draped an arm over Adam Badeau's shoulder. The guest he had invited. Of course. How had she not known? Her brother looked over, raised the waving baby higher in his arms, and nodded at her and the sisters. Ursula's love for him took on a new dimension. And it burned brighter, more protective. Her brother, too good for this imperfect world.

The sisters watched her until her eyes returned to them and stilled on their small circle alone.

"Glad you got you some powerful menfolk, Miss Ursula," Nima said quietly. "You listen to us good, now."

This was important. "Yes" she assured them quietly, "I am listening."

Dibb began. "He coming for you."

Dread circled Ursula's heart. "Who?" she asked.

"Second Master."

Ursula remembered their secret name for him. She was Miss Ursula, her brother Young Master Jon, their mother always and forever Mistress. Her father had never been called Master, he had forbidden it. He was always Captain Henry, his seafaring days name. Still, once her mother remarried, Magnus Kingsley became Second Master, behind his back, in the shadows of the house, in the slave quarters, where she and Jonathan were allowed, sometimes, to dwell.

"The night of your betrothal party, Miss." Nima drew her back into their shared pasts, "Our Abda said Second Master had that look and warned us, so we took to the woods. We knew enough to get away. We knew enough by then. But you did not. And you were the one who crossed him that night , by saying no to marrying his foolish cousin."

Dibb took in a shuttering breath. "We did not think he would, to you."

"To you, Miss Ursula, else we would of warned you," Nima said softly.

"No, no," Ursula whispered. "It is I who am sorry you were treated in such a way in my home. I was a silly girl. With no knowledge of such things. I am so sorry."

Dibb frowned. "You were a child, Miss. Nothing to be sorry for."

"And you did not slander Sling, when Second Master tried to blame it on him. It would have killed Mama, to lose our brother," her sister assured Ursula.

"And she would have, soon, lost him."

"…to Munson's bloodhounds, and the noose. Our Sling could not stand no more, Miss. No more of not being able to protect us from that man."

Dibb patted Ursula's tightly clasped hands. "We were mighty glad he stole himself away that night."

Ursula nodded. "As am I. But my stepfather, he said—"

"That Sling was caught and slaughtered by him. Mama told us."

"Another burden on you, Miss, before you sent away to the holy sisters place."

Dibb resumed the sisters' story, "Second Master hired us out downriver soon after."

"Couldn't sell us, as we belonged to your mama. But hired us out as fancy chefs, where they didn't have the sense to know we was just good eaters who watched in hopes of leavings."

Nima's eyes narrowed. "Wouldn't allow any word or contact back to Mary's Land."

Dibb grunted. "He done punished my mama and yours, we're of a mind."

"Don't like bonds of love."

"Only the money bonds he fancies, that one."

Nima smiled. "Well, you got you yourself your own money now, Mama says. And you got yourself a fine family."

"In danger, maybe," her sister warned. "We will not fail you, even if he got other bad business, and is not looking for you. Have a care, Miss Ursula, because he be in your city."

Ursula's breath caught. "How do you know this?"

"Don't let this free place in Brooklyn deceive you, Miss," Nima assured her. "Outside Weeksville we keep a good eye, ear."

"And nose better than Munson's bloodhounds. We know the Yankee soldiers held onto Second Master for a slave catcher for a while down in the Southland. But they traded him away, on account of that serpent's tongue of his that once caught your mama in its spell. He knows folk will ransom him here, too. Powerful folk who get paid when the slave ships get outfitted right here in this city, bound for Africa, then Cuba. Same folk your daddy and Captain Kane fought all they lives against. Slavers."

Both women spit on the ground.

"Folk like Second Master been grabbing slave and free and runaway, to bring them way downriver to New Orleans and Texas," Nima explained.

"He sometimes travels to this city. Dibb continued. "He and a woman you know, from your holy days. She in the church, like you was."

Ursula gasped. "Sister Philomena?"

"If that one, she goes by Mrs. Charles now, working as a cook. Heard of her in our circles. Your one-eyed Irish man, he shot one of her kin. Shot him dead, in Washington City."

"Yes."

"Well, they both in the Northland," Dibb pronounced.

"Up to no good," her sister declared.

"Looking to bring the Union down." North country is full of rebel spies. They all over, Miss Ursula."

Dibb nodded. "All over, like the train tracks that move them. Weeksville might be the one place they ain't. 'Cause they don't think a place like this possible.

That is how we can talk plain here. And this is what we figure. If they find you here, they be hunting for your man. For you."

Ursula felt that sensation that had overtaken her before, that paralysis. Silencing her. Making the tips of her fingers feel frozen. The thaw stated when Dibb and Nima reached out, took her hands between theirs.

"We will keep watch, Miss Ursula," Nima assured her. "Rest easy. We learn more, we will bring you word."

"I do not deserve you," she whispered, wiping her eyes with the backs of her hands like when they were all children together. "Thank you."

Chapter Eighteen ~ Rowan

Rikers Island

September 1864 ~ Presentation of colors

The day was clear and bright, with wind blowing breezes off the East River. Rowan could forget, sometimes, the teeming metropolis just across the water and south of Rikers Island. He'd imagine himself back at the farm of the three Maries, or back further, to County Leitrim and the headwaters of the Shannon. He was a farm boy at heart, as were the soldiers in his care. Today their superiors were about, watching his men parade, looking for any signs of imperfection in march, in dress, in decorum with their visitors.

Ursula had blossomed in her city life, and with her friends had brought culture and education and kindness and beauty to their campground. With her presence and quiet work among them, at first. And then with the others, all these who bore witness today: the sculptor happily sketching the parade formations, the farmers of Brooklyn led by the Henson family, with their baskets of fruits and vegetables, their handcarts loaded with gifts of preserves for the soldiers to enjoy, and cakes and pies for the picnic after today's graduation ceremony. They even had their poet in Mr. Whitman, scribbling his ode to this place of harmony after the horror of the summer of '63's massacre.

Ursula, Mrs. Selby and her daughter Penina sat watching, their laps festooned with late summer wildflowers their besotted drummer boys had gathered from the camp's outskirts.

And oh, the pure joy that beamed from Henry clapping his hands for all. A year's survival in this world, their son had achieved. He had even taken a few steps all on his own. Was there ever such a child?

The father's pride had caught Rowan by surprise. He expected to be visited by the love, devotion and protection that he'd sensed from his own parents. But presiding over Ryan and Orla Buckley's love was a sense of foreboding, a shielding of themselves. And fear. Fear of the fact that their sons and daughters were children and so could be taken away by a fall, a sickness, a walk too deep into the woods or too far into the pond. That shielding barrier was there so they could recover when one was lost, Rowan supposed now. He and his siblings did not have this protective shielding. The Buckley children lived in wild exuberant love for each other, as if in their youth and beauty, what could be lost?

Then An Gorta Mor, the Great Hunger struck them all down, except for him.

He was now in a new world, where a father might even expect his children to survive, and thrive, and outlive him.

Rowan had no such expectations for his men, for their families. After the fuss of this day, he would lose them to their new officers, ones who had not grown up with negro people, both free and enslaved, as he had in Quebec and Jonathan had on Maryland's eastern shore. Most of the officers had not learned to respect these men, honor their struggle, their hard-won freedom and dignity. For the men marching in beautiful formations Rowan felt the foreboding of his parents. Circumstances and people out of his control were about to come into their lives, along with the re-maining battles of this too-long war.

Today they had brought the city to their training island. Because word had escaped, after the first waves of volunteers had proved themselves valiant, time after time. Too many people. How had they all received passes to be here? He needed to protect his men, their families. This was supposed to be their day, for their farewells. Not this time. Politicians, local, state and federal were here, bringing along their entourage of followers. And representatives of the charitable organizations who had financed their teachers and doctors and craftsmen, all well-intentioned, and welcomed on other Sundays, but today? Too crowded, too impossible to sift through for the ones here to sell snake oil, to take advantage of his men.

And, recording it all, the newspapermen.

The Army spent days constructing grandstands, stringing patriotic bunting. Had they finally realized what these men were going to achieve? That they were going to save their precious union? Did they want their own credit in the bloody business?

A newspaperman approached, holding up two ink-stained fingers, as if Rowan was a cabman he was summoning for a ride. Was he from the Herald or the Times or Evening Post? At least no one from the Caucasian Times was here. Think, Rowan chided himself. He recognized the face. They had been introduced earlier in the day. And his commanders had ordered him to answer all of the scribblers' questions. But Rowan could not even remember the man's name. He had evaded this one's company twice. It was not going to be possible now. His commander looked up from his conversation with Jonathan, with an unspoken demand: stay put. The correspondent approached, as casually disheveled as his men were pressed and polished.

"They acquit themselves well."

"Yes, sir."

"But will they fight, or turn cowardly tail and run, on the battlefield?"

Eyes straight. "I have every confidence in their ability, sir."

"The city fathers discussed a march up Broadway. Thank God they are not parading around our city with those rifles. I know many Irish would slice them open with their pikes."

"Know? Or know of, sir?"

"Oh, I mean no offense to you personally, Captain Buckley,"

Tabarnac! The man remembered his name.

"I must say I feel a little squeamish myself," he continued, "knowing all too well the stories of our Nat Turner and Mad John Brown and the San Domingo years. So many murderous slave revolts. How do you sleep among them, Captain? You are so outnumbered."

"By whom?"

"Whom?"

"Aye. Which ones? Your spineless cowards or your fierce murderers, sir?"

His commander heard and winced. He sent Jonathan over. That was not going to help.

"Ah," the reporter said. "Together, now. The two officers of whom we have heard tales. The two who love them."

"Are we not commanded by our Bible to love each other, Mr. Pressart?" Jonathan said, smiling his most charming smile. And he had remembered the bastard's name. "Would you like to join us for the afternoon's entertainments? You'll find neither cowards or murderers here, but you will hear some fine fiddling, and renditions of Mr. Foster's songs by New York's finest patrol officer, our Harrigan. Sergeant!" he called Sling away from his mother's ten-layer caramel cake, "would you steer our esteemed Mr. Pressart toward the musical entertainments?"

Gone, at last. Rowan spit on the ground. "You'd think the heroism displayed at Fort Wagner would have shut such fools down."

Jonathan laughed his bitter laugh. "Colonel Shaw flying past the ramparts into heaven and his Boston Abolitionist sainthood? I think not. Even the martyr's horse got fuller mention in the newspapers than the troops he commanded. Each regiment, battalion and squad we send out from this place will have to prove itself separately and to the satisfaction of idiots who happen to have white skin."

"Oh, aye."

Rowan felt Jon's hand at his shoulder. "Buck up, kin. It could be worse. We could be training a rabble of frightened draftees or paid-off replacements biding their time before they desert our ranks. These men have fire. They know what they are fighting for."

Rowan watched Ursula plunk out her piano keys for the banjos' tunings. The policeman Harrigan was at her side, fresh from his all together too passionate rendition of "Jeannie with the Light Brown Hair." Rowan's fingers gravitated toward the penny whistle in his pocket. It was going to be a grand afternoon, if he could get lost in her, in the music they made together, in the laughter.

"If only we had the power to get them all home, Jonathan," he said quietly.

"Now, then. Not a one of us is able to work miracles. You know that. Now do not look so sad when your eyes are feasting on my sister, or she will succumb to her fears again and think you are looking to trade her in."

"What are you saying?"

"Only what Marie Agathe tells us— she has taken to her fretting."

"Fretting? Holy Mother of God." Rowan grunted. "How more soundly might I kiss that woman?"

Her brother grinned. "'Kiss,' is it?"

"I should have known this 'simple information gathering' being pressed upon us would undo my happy home."

"Tell her more of it, Rowan."

"And entangle her in this web of ours?"

"What is worse? Unless, or course, you do not trust her."

"Of course, I trust her."

"She has an ever-widening circle of friends. She may be of help."

"Do you hear yourself?" Rowan whispered fiercely. "The federals are seeking her out. For treason."

"They are seeking out my sister, your wife. Not the charming widow Mrs. Major, who is much too free with her favors towards you, one of her many suitors."

"Aye." He frowned. "And she is the one fretting?"

"You are a man, in a man's world. One that is indulgent, even approving of your dalliance with a defenseless war widow, in this godless city. You have freedoms she cannot even imagine. Of course she frets."

"How do you see so clearly through her eyes?"

His brother-in-law laughed. "We are kin, Rowan," he said. His eyes were uncharacteristically sober. And seemed, suddenly, to have been touched by his sister's habitual sadness.

Penina

Mrs. Major chose the right hat today— the deep lavender one with the silk primroses, to go with the summer silk striped yellow and aniline dyed silk purple dress. How well it picked up the golden lights in her brown hair and eyes. Perfection. Penina found she liked sculpting the widow's appearance, even though she would not agree to try on the latest Parisian gorded corset because it rose high, causing too much difficulty when feeding her baby.

Penina had learned that Mrs. Bell, who was Mrs. Major's friend and confidante had, when enslaved, managed the tresses of fine ladies of Maryland's Eastern shore. Mrs. Bell agreed to fashion Penina's hair in the latest style after her 'Miss Ursula' had waved the curling iron away that morning, preferring her simple snood. That was how Penina, who had chosen a cream-colored bodice over her best maroon silk skirt, now wore her tresses carefully turned and placed over her shoulder with a comb. By some magic concoction that went from Mrs. Henson's fingers through Penina's hair, the curls remained coiled through this day's heat, and made her smell pleasantly of rosewater.

"That's our Bibi's hoo-doo," Sergeant Henson's little girls had confided in her, giggling about the magic that came out of Mrs. Bell's "hair elixir" jar.

At the widow's quiet bidding, the soldiers had hauled a piano out of the officers' quarters. Penina watched Mrs. Major provide much of the beat behind The Arkansas Traveler. She fit in as well with these rough and ready men, their families and their wild, percussive dance tunes as she did at the Booth Family salons playing her carefully noted sheet music of Chopin nocturnes. Even her mother had joined the circle and danced, led by Sergeant Harrigan. Penina wanted to join. She wondered if she could learn the dance. But no one took her hands, pulled her out on the grass, not even the shy drummer boys. She'd never learned how to play an instrument, not even a button accordion or small guitar. She was busy helping Papa to sell them. She felt invisible, even among all the bright silk flowers in her basket. Her skill with them she suddenly thought useless and childish.

As they concluded, Captain Buckley placed his tin whistle back into his coat's pocket and took the still clapping baby from Sergeant Kingsley's arms. Mrs. Major's sea captain friend flexed this fingers after keeping up with the younger musicians with his squeezebox. The children skipped about, not yet ready to stop the merriment.

"Thirsty, Miss Penina?" the small voice asked.

"Why, yes I am, Tate."

"You take care of Miss Ursula. I take care of you. How's that?"

"Why that is a grand idea, sir."

The drummer ran to get her refreshment.

Penina watched Mrs. Major pull down her wrinkled inner sleeves to her wrists, ignoring the line of six silk covered buttons. He was right. That woman needed her help, again. If only she took as much care with her appearance as she did with her musical skills. Penina reached into her basket and approached, handing her an eagle-painted fan.

"Here. Cool yourself, Mrs. Major, and allow me to set you to rights," she offered.

"However did I ever keep myself together without you?"

"Hmmm. I suspect you never did."

Mrs. Major laughed and her overheated flush deepened, despite her waving the fan at a furious pace.

"Stop that! You are signaling that you are engaged."

"Oh yes, quite right."

She slowed the pace.

"Now you say that you are married!"

"Oh. Oh, yes." Ursula giggled and drew her closed fan across her eyes, signaling that she was sorry, then laughed again, wide and loud and not ladylike at all, but revealing perfect teeth. Was there anything about her, besides her indifference to the proper adornments of clothes and hair, that was not perfect?

The banjo player arrived with lemonades for them both. Tate was a few steps behind. He turned and disappeared back between two strollers.

Mrs. Major spun around on the piano stool. "Oh, thank you, Corporal Lewis. I'm afraid my beautiful fan reveals all but is of little use at procuring us refreshment."

That laugh again.

"Mrs. Major," Penina summoned, "I wonder which of us is still shy of fifteen years? Kindly wear your gloves and open your parasol, the sunlight grows more direct."

Her mother would not approve of Penina speaking to an elder in such a fashion. But Mrs. Major never seemed offended. Well, they were out of her mother's hearing, as she was busy talking with her policeman.

And now Ursula was having trouble opening her parasol.

"Oh, the bother!" she cried out.

"Fashion is all about enduring difficulty for beauty's sake, Mrs. Major," Penina claimed, sounding ridiculous, even to her own ears.

But Ursula only laughed. "I'm afraid my beauty shall have to emanate from my fondness of you," she said.

"You can be most exasperating, but I am fond of you, too."

The woman's breathing hitched in her throat. She covered Penina's hand with her own. She'd forgone every ornamentation except her wedding ring, which was simple with a small blue stone, so out of style that even older matrons were having theirs remade with more gems.

"Oh, Penina. That makes my heart take flight."

"Now, do not render us both teary-eyed, I do not have your new mother excuse."

That set them to laughing together, which in the rising heat of the day would probably make their faces shine with sweat. It was certainly attracting her mother's attention from gathering children in front for their own dress parade. But Caroline Selby, whose wedding ring was every bit as simple, only shook her head, as if she had two silly daughters and there was no help for it.

Why, Penina wondered? Why was she so important to the widow, with all her gifts and admirers?

Penina's fan, the last of her father's inventory, had yet to be decorated, but there was no more time. She'd been mixing paints and guiding the soldier's wives, mothers and sweethearts' hands. She had left her own fan at the bottom of the box: this one—pearl colored and handled, its lace of surprising quality. It was almost like a fond kiss from her father, lying there. It did not even need airing, to rid it of the smoke of that horrible summer day.

"Oh, Penina," Ursula said, looking over Penina's shoulder as she opened it before her face. "How beautiful."

"But I have not painted it."

"Because you were too busy thinking of others. Now it is a reward for your selflessness. No need to guild that lily. It is perfect as it is."

"That is something Mama would say."

"What a lovely compliment. Thank you." She glanced up beyond them. "Oh, look how Henry enjoys the curving paths the children guide him through."

The baby was indeed chortling as Mrs. Henson's two granddaughters led him towards them. His lace gown had a muddied edge, like that on his mother's skirts. Oh what would either of them do without her?

Penina overheard the newspaperman lean over the sketch artist's shoulder.

"A good likeness of our mysterious war widow. sir. And perhaps the delightful lass at her side is her sister?"

"Possible. Yes, I would say quite possible."

Delightful lass? Not bothersome child, but sister? They meant her. That was surely thanks to Mrs. Major's urgings that Mama allowed her full hoops at last, in the new pyramid shape that allowed a train in the rear… the length of a woman's skirt, not a girl's.

Ursula was gentle and good, like Mama. Penina felt small within both their shadows. Stop frowning, she told her Blue Devils. No shadows. She was basking in her friend's reflected glow.

And being immortalized by the sketch artist of the New York Times, who could have left her out of his portrait. She switched her hold on the fan to her left hand, then waved her father's gift before her face, signaling that she was desirous of making his acquaintance.

The artist smiled.

Jonathan

Jonathan stilled his restless leg by force of will. He did not like the so-called gentlemen of the press here, any more than Rowan did. Especially among the families of the men pic-nicing in their finest clothes. Beautiful families, about to be shredded by war.

Penina and her mother had brought boxes of their wares. They had joined the women and girls festooning hats and hair ornaments with silk birds and flowers. Now they were waved fans painted with American flags, eagles, and shields of liberty. Very patriotic, and all for the union.

There was a story in that, of course, but one that would be ignored. None of the newspaper men were talking with the soldiers' women and children. They were looking for society matrons, the rich wives and daughters of war profiteers, shipping and railroad owners. Just as they talked only to the white officers, not to Rowan's Black sergeants and corporals, or to the enlisted.

But a number of the blasted sketchers did not follow suit. They were seated on the hill, their pencils blazing. They exaggerated the African features of his soldiers and their families to outlandish proportions, for the self-satisfied enjoyment of their uptown readers. They did the same with New York's Irish. Damnation. His men would have been mighty chieftains in the lands of their ancestors. So would Baby HRB.

Jonathan would have driven every last scribbler off the field. But he was not in charge of the day. Their presiding officers wanted their own efforts recorded, wanted the newspaper readers to know that Lincoln's quota was being filled. Adam Badeau had even brought the Times' best artist. He was capturing a decent likeness of Ursula and Penina sitting together, as they watched Ada and Kali dote on Henry, helping his little feet tread across paths they wound for him in the dirt.

Penina slipped her gloved hand through his sister's arm, which seemed to please Ursula immeasurably. The sketcher captured the pleasure they took in each other's company.

Jonathan was pleased too, he realized. The once annoying child was charging ahead toward her womanhood, and toward proving herself useful to those without her advantages. And he was always grateful to anyone who could bring a smile to Ursula's face. That gratitude and the sale of his best racing horse had gained him a brother-in-law, after all.

Yes, he had to finally admit he had a growing fondness for Penina Selby, despite their rocky beginnings. She waved her fan at him in one of her nonsense flirtations. She remained a silly thing. But he had seen her grief at her father's passing, and it had reminded him of his own when he watched his mother sicken and die.

Aaron Shulmann recognized Jonathan's childhood desperation when they whisked Ursula away. He somehow found her, out there in the wide world. Jonathan was sure, even as a child, that the peddler went everywhere, providing more than pins and needles, fans and mechanical wonder toys. He could look into hearts with those deep-set eyes. And he had found Ursula, and brought her comb, so that she would not forget her brother, or his promise to get her out before that convent swallowed her completely.

Aaron Shulmann's eyes bore into Jonathan's soul in the last moments of the man's life. Well, Mr. Shulmann, Jonathan thought, Ursula and I have returned the favor you once did for a lonely little boy and his banished sister. We have found your wife and daughter and made them part of us.

The storekeeper had claimed that he was indebted to Ursula. How? Jonathan turned the puzzle over in his mind again. Would he ever know?

Ursula's lawyer Mr. Gardner appeared out of nowhere, shoving a ribbon-tied artist portfolio into his hands.

"Here, you great fool."

"Now what have I done?"

"I had to pay that popinjay three months of his salary for this."

Jonathan slipped the ties open. The portfolio held the finished portrait of his sister and her protégée. He grinned. "I am deeply touched, sir. A fine memento of the day."

"I did not purchase it for you, but to keep it out of print."

"Oh. Oh, I see. Of course."

"Who invited all these people of the press?"

"Not Captain Buckley or I, sir. We are lowly officers who actually work with the training battalions. You will have to go higher up to find your culprits."

Mr. Gardner grunted.

"My sister's face was last recorded as a daguerreotype before she entered the convent, Mr.

Gardner," Jonathan tried to assure him. "She is much changed since. No one would recognize her from an image so distant in time."

"The government spy agencies have descriptions of her. Given to them by the damned detective agencies before them. And she is a striking woman, despite her own efforts to appear plain."

"Ah yes. That inner glow of hers has cost me more than a few dollars to achieve her safety. We are kindred spirits in our expensive protection. My sympathy."

"Hang your sympathy. And your thanks. It will be added to my monthly retainer."

Jonathan grinned. "My sister has paid for her own portrait? You sir, are a cad."

He looked over to where Rowan was standing too close to his wife and whispering at her ear. Good God, had he just nibbled at the lobe?

Yes, the lawyer had seen it too. He heaved a heavy sigh. "No cad, sir. I am merely a man thoroughly exhausted by your family," he claimed. "Now, make sure that sketcher does not wander back. For I must negotiate a ridiculously under-market value rental agreement between your sister and that headstrong little hornet's mother."

Ursula

Lucius Kane's seamen crew stood at attention, honoring the soldiers, before throwing their caps in the air and giving out three cheers. Henry was still clapping in delight as he approached them.

"This island should always be remembered for the men trained here," he said. "They are going to turn the course of the war."

"What a splendid idea, Captain Kane," she agreed. "Perhaps it could be dedicated as such—to honor their part in freeing themselves and bringing our country together again. This island should belong to them and their families forever in some way, so that their sacrifices are never forgotten. Yes. I must talk with Mr. Gardner."

"Ursula," he warned. "You are planning something again."

"Of course I am. But Atlanta has fallen, giving us hope that the war will be over soon. So, for the future, not now. Now I am a quiet-living matron from Gramercy Park, remember?"

"It is not I who forgets."

"I do not forget. I merely hand ideas to Mr. Gardner."

"Ideas? Schemes, Ursula Martin."

How bittersweet her birth name sounded on his lips. A tribute to her father, his dearest friend. She lost the name when the man her mother's enslaved people called Second Master insisted that both she and Mama take on his, blighting all their lives in the process. She could not rid herself of the memory of his touch. Not since Dibb and Nima had traced him to her city. And Sister Philomena. Would she even know the woman without her nun's habit and veil? Would they know her?

Should she tell her men the rumors that the new Henson refugees had heard? They had their own burdens, their own secrets put upon them by their superiors in this city of sedition. What could they do about it?

Smile. But she no longer felt safe here, on Rikers Island, surrounded by her husband, her brother, and men and women who would put their hand in the fire for her. Because of all the strangers pouring out of the city who had joined them today.

Her men were jittery too.

Well, stay behind her deep-sided bonnet. She would not switch to more fashionable hats, as Penina urged, because they revealed too much of her face. She must remain hidden among any who were strangers. And keep the baby sitting on her knee safe.

Her father's friend was watching her. She smiled broadly. "Oh, if you wish, call my notions schemes, Lucius. But is it not beneficial to assign a man's name to any plan or project to have it more easily accomplished?"

"Mr. Gardner tells me your colorful projects have caused you to become his only client."

"Now, is it my fault that Mr. Gardner has been such a good manager that my inheritance has grown so? Besides, it is past time his clerks are given more responsibility over his other clients' interests. He must leave those diligent fellows room to fly on their own. None of us lives forever."

He sighed. "Not even your rapidly aging godfather."

"Oh, sea captains of great moral consequence are quite exempt from the natural order, my darling. Who else will teach our babies to swim?"

From her lap, Henry chortled. Captain Lucius Kane sighed in defeat. "Against two sets of the Martin dimples, I am powerless."

Magnus

Kane. What was he doing here? He should have worked harder to kill the man long ago. It would have cast suspicion, of course, if both seamen had drowned, both experienced swimmers. He liked killing Henry Martin by way of the water, letting the fishes destroy all evidence. There was an inquiry, insisted upon by the grieving widow. Which he, or course, joined, becoming her hero, and casting suspicion on his friend, thus exiling him from the Eastern shore for years.

Yes, Kane lost out on his chance with her, thanks to the doubts carefully seeded. Gone too long at sea in his own grief helped draw her away. When he returned, she had married, and was bulging with their own brat. And what a mistake that child was— bonding to the women: his mother, his sister and that damned slave instead of to him. His wife only made troublesome, blighted children, no matter who fathered them.

Go away from his failures, concentrate on Kane. Was he a widow hunter now, too? After Mrs. Major of Gramercy Park and her fortune? Her summer bonnet obscured her face, so Magnus concentrated on her trim, girlish figure, the fan dangling from her wrist.

Women and their nonsensical frippery. It was getting exhausting, paying them court.

Even the negro women sported fans here, thanks to Penina Selby and her efforts among them. She and her mother's growing success was putting them further and further out of his reach. It was not his charms failing him, no. It was this damned city, allowing women to gain independence from selling worthless trinkets. And the ones with whom the mother and daughter shared their wares today. Apes, the lot of them, pretending to be real ladies.

He wished to smother them in their abolitionist banners. Along with the pica-ninnies, of course, for nits grow into lice. And why not? Why not call Phil down from Canada, to enlist as cook with one of these damnable charities, fetching forth her apple crisp, slowly and effectively laced with arsenic?

There were more Black soldiers here than he thought possible. He had used the silly girl and her mother to get over to Rikers Island. Now he must gage their numbers, their ability to cross the river to Manhattan. He must report it all back to his friends of the Sons of Liberty, to the Confederate Army of Manhattan. Perhaps they would hatch a new part of their plan.

But for now, he had a new widow to meet.

Chapter Nineteen ~ Penina

"Mrs. Major, may I introduce to you— "

Ursula looked up from the piano. "Who, dear?"

Penina turned. "That's strange. He was standing here a moment ago. And he has been pestering me for an introduction since I told him we were now friends."

"Your Mr. Burwell? Who has such a low opinion of me?"

"The very same. Well, he had a keen interest in the troops as well, so perhaps he is off toward them."

"Who had a keen interest in the troops?" Jonathan demanded.

"Our tenant, Mr. Burwell."

"And what is his business here? How does he make his living?"

"I don't know sir. He seldom resides in his rooms, as he travels. And he often visits with friends when he boards with us."

"Travels? Visits? You have not brought upon this island some charlatan waiting to defraud with false insurance policies or inferior sutler goods I trust?"

"I—" She was not used to Sergeant Kingsley like this, so official and protective of his men. And frowning at her. He was on duty here, not Ursula's carefree friend, and doting uncle to her child. Had she done something wrong? Where was Mr. Burwell, who could answer these questions? "I hope not, Sergeant."

"Well. We'd best hunt him up and have him declare the intention behind his interest."

Sergeant Kingsley placed her hand firmly into the crook of his arm, not taken it as he would a child's, but as if he were escorting a lady. And he was very handsome. All eyes of both soldiers and the city people were on them as they walked. That eased some of Penina's worry.

"There he is, at the dock." She did not point but nodded her head as a lady, not as a child might. "Why is he leaving? He was so adamant about—"

As she raised her arm to wave, her escort took her waist suddenly and placed them both behind an elderberry bush. "Sergeant Kingsley! What are you—"

"Quiet," he warned.

"But I thought you wished to—"

"That is your tenant?"

"Yes, sir."

"His name is not Burwell."

"No?" She grinned. "How exciting."

"Not the word I would use. Listen to me you little flibbertigibbet. I need to know everything he has said to you about Mrs. Major."

"Why not ask him, he stands right there."

"Waiting for a ferry. Because he has discovered her."

"Sergeant Kingsley, you are acting in a very peculiar—"

"Hush," he warned. So Penina held her very breath, and thought it thrilling, to be so still, and in hiding.

"There, gone," he said at last, lifting his head as the small boat headed west. "We have very little time." He took her shoulders between his hands and stared into her eyes. She had never seen him so serious. "He's a danger to her, little bird. A very grave danger. He has been using you to get to her. For a different reason, I suspect, for he had not yet seen her. But now he knows."

"Knows what?"

"Who the widow of Gramercy Park is."

"And who is she?"

"My sister. And I will not lose her ever again." He grabbed her hand exactly like an errant child now. "Hurry. We must find Rowan."

She stood between the two men as they peppered her with questions.

"Did he meet with people in his rooms?"

"No, never."

"What of his clothes, did he change them often? Were they different in character?"

"I do not think so. Mama used to amuse Papa when he was in the hospital, telling him of the quality of Mr. Burwell's brocade waistcoats."

"Your father met this man?"

"No, never. Mama did not rent out the rooms until after the fire."

He looked up at Captain Buckley. "Mr. Shulmann would have known him, Rowan. Mr. Shulmann would have known what had invaded his home."

"Mr. Shulmann? How do you know our other name?" Penina asked, but Sergeant Kingsley's eyes remained fixed on his captain.

"Mark that, brother," he said. "Brocade waistcoats." He closed his eyes, then stared hard at his superior officer. "His hair is longer, more full, than last we saw him, with more silver. So is his beard. A full beard. Trimmed neatly."

"His speech is like yours, Sergeant," Penina sought to help further.

He snorted. "Well, that cannot be helped." A knowing look passed between the men, before a warning one from Captain Buckley. Penina knew now what eye to follow as the source of his expression.

"What do we do?" she asked them both.

"Find him," Sergeant Kingsley answered. "Find his associates. Bring him down."

"Who is he, Sergeant?"

"A hunter, Miss Selby. Of widows, of negroes. You and your mother will be well rid of him. His touch is deadly."

"You have confronted each other before?"

He ignored his commanding officer's pressing hold at his arm. "Many times. He is my father."

"Ostie de colon!" burst from Captain Buckley, before he turned his back on them both.

Penina thought she knew a few blasphemies, but she'd never heard that one. "I think he called me an idiot," Jonathan Kingsley translated for her.

"Our tenant is Ursula's rich father? But I thought—
"

"No, he is not Henry Martin. Your Mr. Burwell is Magnus Kingsley. He is my father only, not Ursula's. God help me."

His friend turned. "He will, Jonathan," he promised softly. "You are your mother's child."

Penina stepped closer and fixed her gaze on the bigger man's good eye. "And who are you, Captain Buckley?"

He remained silent.

But Sergeant Kingsley spoke up. "Our Ursula's husband, if you must know," he said. He shoved his captain's shoulder lightly. "Kindly replace that 'you moron,' look, brother. Penina has done us a great service. He's here. Right where we can find him."

"First we need to get Ursula and Henry away. Moved. Find Captain Kane. He will help us."

Chapter Twenty ~ Ursula

Rowan paced her spacious front sitting room as if caged in a prison cell. Jonathan, was all stillness, standing at Ursula's side. His hand rested casually at her shoulder. Ursula covered it with her own. How deeply she loved her brother and her husband.

"I have told Penina Selby our true family connections," Jonathan said. "You cannot expect her to keep secrets from her mother."

Rowan continued to pace. "I know, I know." Finally, he stopped as if commanded to halt by General Grant himself. "There is no help for it," he declared. "We must take both Selbys into our confidence. A partial confidence," he amended.

Jonathan squeezed her shoulder. "Agreed. Soon. Let us visit with them tomorrow. Not at the house, at their shop."

"Good." Ursula breathed out.

"Good?"

"Of course, my loves. It has been a great burden not to treat them like part of our family."

"You express no such trepidation about the Booths," Rowan observed.

"The Booths? Oh, Edwin is a dear, and he tries to keep me isolated from their family squabbles, serious, trite and political. In return, my hands provide soothing musical interludes for his melancholy. For the wider Booth family, I am also pair of hands, a listening ear. And they are contacts into a social world whose inhabitants will purchase and proclaim the beauty of Selby's Hats and Lady's Accessories."

Jonathan's eyebrow quirked up. "Why, sister. How very transactional New York City has made you."

Her husband's expression was more full of wonder. "Truly, 'Sula?"

"Truly. And they are actors, my darlings. Have you seen how much they eat?"

The men laughed aloud. My, that was a lovely sound.

***

I am so sorry, my dear," Ursula sought to assure her friend.

Caroline looked past the worktable strewn with pearls and silk butterflies. "Mr. Burwell threatens you? Is that the reason for your false name, and false widowhood?"

"I am afraid so."

"Please forgive us for not telling you sooner," Ursula asked.

It seemed Caroline's daughter required no such apology. "Is it not wonderful, Mother? A great mystery is solved. Our Ursula is the lady crucial to papa's happy death. And she is not a widow at all, as Captain Buckley is the only one of her beaus that she kisses for a reason. He is her husband!"

"Wonderful, yes," her mother said, smiling as if her heart was breaking at the same time. She stared at their hands.

Rowan came between them, searching Caroline Selby's placid face. "We have confronted the man before. He is dangerous."

"What can I do to help you?"

"Keep up your cordial relations with your tenant, Mrs. Selby, so that we may—"

"I am afraid that is not possible, Captain."

"I realize this request is an affront to your honest nature, but—"

"Captain Buckley, Mr. Burwell is gone."

"Gone?"

"With all his possessions, by the time we arrived home from the festivities last evening. He left us only this note."

She brought it from her apron's pocket. Rowan took it. Both men leaned over it, reading until Jonathan's head came up.

"May we check his rooms?"

"Yes. Penina, here are the keys." She drew them from her gown's deep side pocket and placed them in her daughter's open palm. "Will you accompany the gentlemen to—"

"Of course, Mama. I am closing the shop first. Sit with our Ursula, drink your tea. You don't look well."

***As the men left with Penina, Ursula felt a strange fear at being alone with a woman who had shown her nothing but kindness. Because her friend's eyes were bright with unshed tears.

She finally spoke. "I am sorry for any part we played in your distress, Mrs. Major," she whispered hoarsely.

"Please, Caroline. My name is my husband's — Mrs. Buckley. But make me Ursula again. Forgive me."

"There is nothing to forgive."

"There is. I should have told you the circumstances of my life in New York sooner. I should have placed more trust in you. My brother and husband advised against it. But I do not put any blame on them, understand me. They seek my protection always and

above all. And of our little innocent. We will do anything to keep our Henry safe. You have a precious
child. You understand this."

"I do. I cannot lose my daughter, Mrs. Major."

"Has our plight awakened a dormant fear in you?
The fear of every woman left a widow with her child?
Separation? Please understand. This shop will pros-
per, I know it. And our Mr. Gardener will not tolerate
any mother and child separation for either of us."

"He cannot accomplish this miracle for us both."

"Why not? Has not our benefactor—"

"Enough dissembling! You are my benefactor. Mr.
Gardner works at your behest."

"Well…I— yes." This was not how Ursula had pic-
tured this moment in her mind. Not al all.

"You have been trying to buy our affection from
our beginnings."

"No. Oh, my dear—"

"No more 'my dears' out of you. You cannot buy
her."

"Buy her?"

"Penina is my daughter!"

"Of course she is. I seek only your family's friendship."

"Impossible. You are a deceitful woman. I want
nothing to do with you."

"Caroline. Look at me. Please."

Caroline Selby stared into her lap. "And see that gush of tears you use to achieve your ends?"

"I am powerless over my— my gushing. Surely you remember how it was when you, yourself—"

"Get out! Get out of my shop while it is still mine."

Mr. Gardner stood in the doorway. "It will always be yours, Mrs. Selby. As will your garden plot and your home."

Penina entered the room, followed by Rowan and Jonathan.

"Ours? Do you hear Mama? Oh, Mr. Gardner, you are the best of men."

"No, Miss Selby. It is Mrs. Buckley who has divested certain of her holdings to benefit your family."

"Ursula? Is this true?"

"Yes." She wiped her wet cheeks with the back of her hands. "I am sorry, I am sorry."

Penina knelt at her feet. "It is not only that library room and piano and your fine chinaware, then? You own your house? And ours?" She looked to Mr. Gardner. "And others?" she asked

He nodded.

"Ursula. You are not rich. You are wealthy."

She shook her head. "Not through my own achievements."

"But you have provided our chance, our independence, our comfort. That is your achievement."

"Opportunity. I only sought to provide opportunity. Please forgive me."

Penina squeezed their entwined fingers. "For what? For being the dearest friend we have ever known? That requires no forgiveness, does it, Mama?"

Caroline Selby stared hard at her lap. "We are deeply in your debt, Mrs. Major."

"Mama, she is our Ursula. What is wrong?"

Her mother's lips twitched. "There are so many changes."

"Happy ones, Mama. We have been taken into Ursula's true, mysterious family. These men, her friends, they are her family. They are Baby Henry's father and uncle. This is all so very exciting!"

"Yes. It has quite overwhelmed me."

Chapter Twenty One ~ Rowan

He and Jonathan went into the meeting with a plan. They would keep the generation-older men's attention hopping between them, both the ones who thought them resourceful, and the ones who thought them fools. Perhaps that would force them to regard the substance of their findings, and not their youth or heritage. And always, always, give them time to come up with conclusions, so they could take the credit.

"Well, gentleman. You have discovered the identity of the mysterious Mr. B., leader of the conspiracy band, only to lose the man himself. Did you find anything interesting at his residence?"

Jonathan presented *The Stranger's Handbook to the City of New York* on the polished veneer pedestal table. Each of their superiors thumbed through its worn pages.

"A tourist guide? For his compatriots and himself, no doubt. Amusements, while biding their time," one decided.

"Enjoying themselves, in the big city," another agreed, disgusted.

"Useless," concluded another.

It did not matter, Rowan thought. He and Jonathan had already committed to memory the places marked with crude red stars. The Astor Hotel, Barnum's American Museum, with its waxworks room citation underlined twice, The statue of Washington, City Hall Park.

Rowan stepped forward. "We also discovered a list, in his room's fireplace. Burnt at the edges. Of addresses."

"Any commonality?"

Jonathan's turn to speak up. "All of them are hotels, sirs."

"Where the other conspirators resided?"

"Most likely," a compatriot agreed. "And under false names, like him."

"Alerted by Burwell. And all cleared out by now," said another.

Their superiors laughed off a note made in the margins: "These Yankees," it read, "will learn what it is to incur the enmity of a proud and chivalric people."

"The ravings of blowhards."

"And so, your list is also useless."

Rowan spoke. "Perhaps not, if he thought to burn it. Do you think, sirs?"

He and Jonathan had visited all the hotels. His turn. Question. Rowan saw his brother-in-law's struggle. How could he make it into a question, a mystery, for them to solve?

"Most were up and down Broadway, sirs," he blurted out.

"So?" one asked.

"They form a path, you see."

"And?"

"A path of destruction if someone decided to strike a match on a windy night."

The men circled them both now. "Are you saying that you have thwarted a plot, by chasing the mysterious Mr. Burwell and his cohorts from the city before this imagined plot became reality?"

"No sirs, not at all," Rowan tried to quell their anger.

Their leader stopped. "Still, we ought to maintain supervision of refugees' southern states, of course."

"Of course, of course," his cohorts approved.

"And telegraph the mayors of Buffalo, Detroit, Chicago…"

"Cleveland?"

"Excellent idea, Clive. Yes, Cleveland too. Tell them we have uncovered a rebel conspiracy to burn northern cities. Adam Badeau will use the influence he has at the Times. And with Grant. And his connections will plant the stories in the newspapers of Cleveland, Boston, Buffalo. He's crafty. They will never know the rumor's origin. That should bring in the troops."

"Will it?"

"With Election Day approaching? President Lincoln will make sure of it."

Jonathan stole a look at Rowan, who nodded. Success. Even with Jonathan not figuring out how to question it out of them.

Perhaps they could slip away while the men were congratulating each other. To Ursula's house in Gramercy Park. He could bathe Henry, and eat a bowl of Marie Agathe's pouding chomeur, and make love to his wife. And sleep for a few blessed hours, in the haven of her arms, before he and Jonathan figured out where to send them, to keep them safe. His heart clenched. They would find them. They would find them again. He tried to quell the fear.

One of their scheming superiors lifted his head. "Don your disguises. Time for another visit to the Old Grapevine Tavern for you gentlemen," he decided.

"Now that Mr. B. has a full name. See if you can pick up leavings of their trail."

Jonathan

They stood before the West Side's most notorious roadhouse. Rowan pulled some of his shirt out of his misbuttoned vest.

"Still too neat," Jonathan advised.

He doused it and sprinkled Rowan's unkempt sergeant's coat from the contents of his flask. "There. Better."

Rowan frowned. "It is too quiet."

"We have never arrived this late."

"I don't like you going in there alone."

"We have no MacKneel and Hayes to watch our backs tonight. We need to look out for each other, kin. Regard your timepiece. Give me ten minutes to get a few names, maybe some whereabouts."

Rowan pulled the chain from his vest's pocket. "What if—"

"If I need you before then, I will send someone out."

"Who?"

"A boy on an errand."

"But—"

"Rowan. Wait here."

Jonathan tucked Penina's box under his arm and entered the largely empty barroom. He recognized none of the patrons. The errand boy was not beside the large hearth fire.

The barkeep looked nervous, not his usual convivial self.

"Has Mr. Burwell been in of late?" Jonathan asked.

"You know his name."

"Of course."

"He left a message for you."

"Yes?"

The proprietor wiped the bar. His hands were shaking. "It's out back, salesman."

"The message?"

"The messenger. With the message. You can leave the box."

"But this is my stock and trade."

"Just so. Leave it," he said, almost kindly. "I will keep it for you."

"I think perhaps I shall—"

But two men with brooms flanked him now, ready to sweep him out a series of back ways and yes, into an alley. Without even his box to pitch danger away.

They left him facing the most gigantic man he'd ever seen.

The man pulled off a worn cap. "Don't worry, lad," he said. "I am not to break any bones."

Rowan

Rowan checked his watch, his firearm. Why was he not in there? Because they knew him as the loud-mouth Sergeant being recruited by the likes of Abbot and Cantwell, he reminded himself. His job was gathering names and schemes from them as they pumped him for information about his activities on Rikers Island. And told him of crazy plans he then reported to their superiors.

Jonathan was the salesman with the same accent as their contact Mr. B. Jonathan was now hunting up the whereabouts of his own father.

Was Magnus Kingsley in there? Rowan had met with the man only once. Once was enough to know there was evil between Magnus Kingsley and Ursula. Was it based in his avarice? Kingsley wanted her inheritance, an inheritance that Mr. Gardner had turned into an even greater fortune in this city were everything was for sale. And he was willing to enlist Rowan in his efforts to have his wife declared infirm of mind. Rowan had seen Ursula in her stepfather's presence, seen her eyes go blank, ice over like a sudden frost on a pond.

And Jonathan, his Union soldier son was, of course, a great disappointment to the old slave-stealer. There was no love lost between them. But the man would not harm his own blood, would he?

Of course he would.

Jonathan

The first punch sent Jonathan's teeth through his lip, the second drove him into the building's clapboards and to the ground. The alley tilted. Get up. But he could not find his feet.

The giant cocked his head. "Not a fighting man?"

He spat out the surge of blood. "Oh, I can fight. But I imagine it would be pointless against such a brick wall as yourself."

"I do not like what he said about you. He thought it would enrage me, as if I was some bull seeing red. But a man can't help being what he is."

"Pretty?"

The punisher made a low rumble, which Jonathan presumed to be a laugh. "That's what he told me to destroy. Your smart mouth. Your pretty face. But no bones. Mean cuss, Mr. Burwell is."

"Now, he could have helped being that."

The massive fingers took hold of his hair, pulled him to his feet against the rough clapboard wall.

"You're no yelper," the giant observed. "It is easier with the yelpers. Listen, if—"

"…you release him, now, I will not shoot you."

In the silence that followed, Rowan cocked his revolver.

"That one of Mr. Colt's Baby Dragoons, sir?" the giant asked.

"Side hammer," Rowan corrected.

"Too small to do me much harm, I imagine."

Rowan raised the weapon higher. "Unless you care for your brains."

"What little use they are to me, I do."

He released his hold on Jonathan, whose knees would not work now. No matter, he thought, as Rowan grabbed hold of his coat at the shoulder and backed them out of the alleyway.

The punisher stayed rooted. "I was not going to do him as much harm as was paid for," he said quietly. "A man cannot help—- mind the cat, now."

Jonathan caught sight of the mottled tabby in his peripheral vision and steered his one-eyed kinsman around it.

***

They slipped into Ursula's kitchen and located a bottle of some awful tasting herbal infused whiskey among Marie Agathe's medicinals to dull his pain. It was late and the stone walled room was empty, its fire banked for the night. Well, something was in their favor, Jonathan thought. At least the women were not about, though it left him at the mercy of his brother-in-law's ministrations.

"Leave it to you to find the only soft-hearted rogue in New York," Rowan groused, as he helped remove Jonathan's blood-soaked coat and planted him on a fireside chair. He turned up the oil lamp.

"Keep your head back. Any teeth loosened?"

"No."

"And your jaw?"

"Intact."

Rowan mixed a splash of whiskey in the basin of water and soaked Jonathan's last clean handkerchief. Then he pressed it so hard against the wound that spots danced around his brother-in-law's black curls.

"Jon, stay," Rowan commanded in his captain voice.

Jonathan tried to push his arm away, missed it completely. But he found his voice. "Stop manhandling me."

Rowan grunted and checked under the cloth. "Soaking through. Maybe we should call Ursula."

"No need. Head wounds bleed more. Have we not seen enough of them?"

"Aye, of course."

"We are finished at the Grapevine, Rowan. I even lost the box, and Penina's gee-gaws."

"Never mind. Never mind any of it."

"But we were making progress."

"There, it is stopping at last. Stay still, figgie-fuss."

Ursula appeared in the kitchen doorway in her nightgown and wrapped in her red paisley shawl, a sewing basket under her arm. She joined them, handing Rowan a needle. "Pass it through the lamp's flame, my darling," she instructed, before surveying Jonathan's wound.

"Would you like some whiskey?" she asked, taking her place on the sturdy chair Rowan placed for her.

Jonathan glanced down at the bottle at his feet. "I am a little ahead on that account, sister."

"Two or three stitches should do," she said, as cool as when she was a nursing sister after the Battle of Antietam.

"Will they provide an interesting scar?"

She widened her stance. "I shall do my best."

"You always do."

Once they'd put his feet up on Henry's little stool and placed a blanket to his chin, Rowan stood behind her, slipping his arms about her waist.

"I am not sleeping," Jonathan warned them. "No carnal expressions of Cupid's shafts, you two."

Rowan snorted like a horse. A pleasant sound. Perhaps that was why he tolerated the man, Jonathan thought. But he did not, for once, speak the thought. His sister moved closer to him as her husband poked more heat from the fire.

She squeezed his hand. "Rest," she urged.

"Not yet. Ursula, you must go away from here."

"Why?"

"We thought you would be safe, with him gone."

"I am safe."

"No. He has gone, but left his punishers."

Her hand went to her mouth. "Oh, Jon."

"Yes. I was his target. His very specific target. And I have no fortune to steal."

She was not thinking of her fortune, or of herself, of course. Oh, that soft heart, made softer by HRB, was erupting again. "Stop it," he pleaded, "Look, all my handkerchiefs are waiting for Marie Agathe and washday." He cocked his head toward the laundry basket with the blood-stained linens. "Regardez."

More tears, instead of the laughter he sought. "Rowan," he called for his brother-n law's assistance. "Tell her. She must leave here."

"Hush, now," Rowan said softly as he stroked the side of her face. "You are upsetting your already ornery patient." There, her tears and hiccoughs were finally easing. "Captain Kane will help us get you to the Maries' farm, 'Sula. You and Henry and Marie Agathe. You will be welcome. And you will meet Marie Catherine, who is the best cook of the three Maries, and is so lonely without her sisters. It is not so fine a place as as you are used to here, but—"

"He is going to Canada," Ursula said.

"Why, who supposes this?"

"Dibb and Nima. And they do not suppose. They know."

"They are more than your vigilant guardians," Jonathan realized. "Sister. You have your own spies."

"Yes," she said as if telling him that Penina had made her a new hat. "He will find me there, Rowan, at your beautiful farm in Canada. I will bring death to your family."

"She's right," Jonathan realized.

Her eyes fired with purpose, with her intelligence. "And I will not be parted from you. Mr. Lincoln's first election started the war. The second is coming. Perhaps it will end it. This country, this war, it is mine. It is mine, too."

"As much for you as for us, sister," Jonathan agreed. "They should never have doubted your loyalty, Ursula."

Rowan frowned. "But they did. We must keep you and Henry safe, 'Sula."

"We can hide in plain sight."

"Where?"

"In Weeksville."

"Forgive me, my darling girl," Rowan said gently, "but you will hardly disappear among the faces of Weeksville."

How had they not talked all their dilemmas over with her, their sworn secrets be damned, Jonathan thought. "She's right, brother. That town is invisible to the eyes of the cities of New York and Brooklyn. As is its citizens and all they have achieved. Yes, I am warming to this idea. And those Amazonian daughters of Miriam will guard you and Henry like she-wolves. It is the perfect place."

"If Miriam will allow it," Ursula stipulated.

"Of course she will allow it, we are family."

"Whose family owned hers for generations, you arrogant man."

"Well, yes." He smiled. "We must ask politely, of course."

Chapter Twenty Two ~ Magnus

St. Lawrence Hall, Montreal
October 20, 1864

The actor who had excited his audience hours before with his reading of *The Charge of the Light Brigade* was now slumped in a corner. Well, it was a wonderful performance. Magnus bought him a drink.

The actor raised his glass. "Mr. Burwell, I presume?"

"Among other names."

"Get yourself a Canuck one, sir. Some of us may have to settle here shortly." The actor placed the glass on the table beside him. "Did you purchase my drink, sir?"

"In honor of a stirring rendition."

"Truly? Though I am a mere actor, singing of military exploits, while you associate with the brave members of Morgan's Raiders?"

Even drunk, he was observant, Magnus noted. He must be more careful.

Both the friendly British and the unfriendly French of the city were tolerant of all its American guests—deserters, draftees on the run, escaped prisoners of war. They languished, drank to excess. They relied on spies and counterspies of both sides to feed their bad habits. He was like them, once. Begging his wife for money to feed his gambling, his carousing. Then she and her lawyers turned on him. She did not know her place, just as her slaves did not. But she had money. Money that should have been his, if his was truly a Christian country, where men held dominion over their wives. And daughters.

The actor stood now that the meeting was coming to order.

"It makes little difference, head or tail, for Abe's contract is near up, and whether re-elected or not he will get his goose cooked."

"Yes, yes, take your seat, Mr. Booth," they shouted him down.

Plots to destabilize and terrorize the Union abounded, safely hatched from this neutral ground north of the United States' border. Was Thompson granting money to the mad actor for his own schemes? How many of the plots would be funded, peopled, carried out? A fraction of the total. How many of them even made sense? That is why theirs had to be the most feasible. And effective.

To get the war won, or at least, ended with a truce. On favorable terms for the South. Solidifying a country that could grow. That could become an empire based in slavery, with the negroes back in their proper place.

He raised his hand for attention among this meeting of Confederate officers. most of them closer to his son's age.

Evans noticed at last and brought him forward. Magnus waited until the room was quiet.

"The citizens of New York City will arm themselves and stand ready to defend the liberties of their city against federal tyranny."

"What makes you think so, Mr. Burwell?"

"Our commercial ties, sir. Cotton is king in the factories of the North, and even in abolitionist New England. The bankers have lost their Southern clients. Again, this summer, the hotels are not filled with Southern gentlemen and their ladies, come to shop Manhattan's delights, then have their grand excursions up the Hudson or Connecticut rivers to the falls at Niagara, the gorges of Vermont. The good citizens of America's largest city—"

"Their city, sir. Capitol of the avarice-ridden North. A stinking filthy place, with pick pockets on every corner!"

Maintain calm, Magnus told himself. He was like these hot-headed young men, once. "There is truth in what you say, gentlemen. I am speaking, not of its lower orders, but of those clever enough to lead them. I am speaking of our allies in Tammany Hall, who know how to turn a rabble into an army. They will join with the bankers, the merchants, who miss their Southern friends, and hate this war. If called upon, these allies will do their part."

"And how do you propose that we call them, Mr. Burwell?"

"With fire in the night, sir. Election night."

They moved closer. He had found their attention. He would soon be training his team.

URSULA ~ Election Night ~ Weeksville, Brooklyn

"They're saying that even General McClellan's soldiers voted for Mr. Lincoln over Little Mac," Rowan told her.

Jonathan frowned. "Well, he did bring ballots to them on the field, and approve furloughs for others to go home and vote."

They had brought three of their current trainees, one from New Hampshire and two from Massachusetts, who had cast their ballots for Father Abraham. The citizens of Weeksville shook the men's hands. Children touched the blue sleeves of their uniforms as if they were angel wings.

"The constitution must change now," Miriam said, beaming. "We are not three-fifths of a person. We count."

"And vote," Mr. Bell said.

Ursula placed the small American flag in Henry's hand. To her delight he did not try to eat it, but waved it merrily, imitating the older children in the wagon. Rowan put his penny whistle to his lips, playing *The Battle Cry of Freedom*. Ada Henson took the handle of the wagon, and the parade around the village green was off.

This was so different from election days of her childhood, Ursula thought, wild parties ending in drunken brawls that broke her mother's wine glasses and porcelain ware. She would always remember this one, in the midst of war, her family harbored in this place that held such promise for the future. The voters had re-elected their president. But these people loved him. She hoped Mr. Lincoln would prove worthy of their love.

November, 1864 ~ New York City

Eight men had remained past election day, biding their time, working on producing Phil's formula for Greek Fire, here in this shack recently vacated by the city's poor Blacks to make way for Central Park. Storing it in gallon jars. They worked here deep in the night, then rested in rooms of the best hotels along Broadway. Hotels they would soon destroy. They were growing restless, of course. They were young. But they must not be careless. Not with an explosive that ignited with air.

So many failures. The war was collapsing around him. Richmond and Petersburg were holding out against Grant's forces, but Sherman was ravaging a path from Atlanta to the sea. Uprisings along the Great Lakes' cities had failed. The invasion at St. Albans, Vermont was deemed no more than a bank robbery. Why? Damned slothful, sympathetic Northerners were too content, too far away from the battlefield.

And then, the election. The victors quickly suing for peace was never certain. If Lincoln had not formed his unholy alliance with the War Democrats, if Atlanta had held out, the Confederacy would have recovered, then risen again, expanding its power southward, into the fertile ground of Cuba, of Mexico and Central America. If Atlanta had not fallen.

The last outrage: Their election night plans aborted when telegrams were sent to mayors leading to the New York Times headline: *Rebel Conspiracy to Burn Northern Cities*. Lincoln sent Union troops to guard the polls. Their contacts, even McMaster at the Freeman's Journal and Catholic Digest lost heart. McMaster had promised them an army of Copperheads to take over the city once the fires started. The city voted for McClellan, but the country re-elected that vulgar despot. They had crowned him king.

Well, the troops were gone now, the tension eased. Let them celebrate, let them grow complacent. The biggest prize was still waiting: New York City. They would play on its materialism, its longing to return to being the center of commerce, unimpeded by blockades and shortages. What would the Copperheads do when he set all of Manhattan Island ablaze?

They would, at last, take up arms. Join them. Get behind him, Colonel Burwell. He'd been promised ten thousand. That would be enough.

Back in '61, before the fighting started, New York had voted to become a free city. But once the war was raging Republicans formed their unholy alliance with the masters of commerce. None of his associates in the Kidnapping Club, of course, but the truly wealthy, the factory owners and railroad men. For them, the war was good business. Now he and these young men, they would force the city to become a free state, like the Italian cities of old.

The port of New York would open up England and Europe again to the cotton trade. They would never again even flirt with having Egypt or India provide for their needs. All of Europe would then recognize the Confederacy.

Let abolitionist New England and their empty factories have their precious union, then. They would help deliver New York City to the Confederacy. And when the federals sent over the Black devils training on Hart and Rikers islands to help them, the filthy Irish would complete his work for him and throw the Blacks in the flames. Then they would have nothing but conscripts and mercenaries to fight for their high ideals.

Apes as free citizens! That would work as fortuitously as it had in that cursed San Domingo, poverty-stricken, paying off the French for their war. The South would recover, and rise again, and find the strength to expand through the hemisphere. That was God's will. Not this growing acceptance of their defeat, not God punishing them for their sins.

Atlanta had been burned off the face of the earth. Well. Other cities could burn.

Jacob Thompson's chatter and the infernal misery his bad tooth was giving him brought him out of his reverie.

"The Giantess Anna Swan at the Barnum Museum has a lovely singing voice. And she quotes Shakespeare, imagine."

"I imagine she would make a formidable Lady MacBeth," Jack Headley agreed.

"At three hundred and forty pounds she could do all the killing the play requires herself. Wouldn't need that mealy-mouth speechifying husband of hers at all, eh? Where shall we go tomorrow?" Bob Kenney asked.

"I will consult the *Stranger's Guide*. It has some capital suggestions. Mind the fire. Jacob, we need more wood. Are you falling asleep?"

"Who can sleep when there are so many amusements at every hour in this city? And our hotel has a barber shop within that can accommodate sixteen gents at a time."

Had he been left with a crew of college boys out for a city romp? That hurt worse than his molar. They might blow themselves up before their incendiaries reached the targets. Perhaps he needed to engage the services of a chemist for final storage, Magnus thought. Yes. Once he thought of a way that would not arouse suspicion.

***

"A gross of the glass vials, you say?"

"Exactly."

"I might have that many stored away. I'm retired, you see. Who sent you to me?"

"Why, Mr. Olmstead himself, sir. He remembers your assistance when he was designing the park with Mr. Vaux."

"That was most kind of him." The chemist frowned. "You must instruct all users of its properties once they are filled. As soon as they come into contact with air, they will explode."

"I have already done that, sir."

"And it must be stored with safety in mind, separated, and with utmost care."

"I understand. They will be placed to blast away small obstructions…a recalcitrant tree root, a boulder broken up, you see?"

"And to what office of the Central Park Commission do I send the bill?"

The bill. Of course, the bill. "Are you aware of the many private donations toward aspects of the grand effort?"

"Oh, yes. The acting Booth brothers upcoming performance is to raise money for a statue of William Shakespeare in the park. Imagine, all three of them sharing the same stage right here in our city."

"Exactly. Well, I represent an anonymous donor who would like to make a gift of these vials. In order to make more efficient a particularly difficult section of the construction."

Had he explained that part already? Magnus felt his mouth aching, despite Phil's poultice and the whiskey. Perhaps he should have the damned tooth pulled. The chemist cocked his head, staring him down. "An interesting use of the substance," the man observed.

"Yes, things we learn in wartime, put to a much better use, would you not agree?"

"Humph. Only if they allow everyone to use the park. If it does not become for rich people in their carriages, as it seems to be now."

"Exactly. This is an experiment to hasten along the park's completion and open it for use of all."

"And, this friend of the construction? He will assure payment?"

It pained him, but Magus smiled his most charming smile. "In advance. Now, if you'd like."

"That would be acceptable. And I can recommend a dentist to see to that enflamed tooth, sir."

Chapter Twenty Three ~ Penina

The Winter Garden Theater, New York City

November 25, 1864

There was not a moment in Penina's life that had been more exciting. And this one was compounded by remembering her first time at a theater— attending *The Merchant of Venice* with her papa. She was only ten, but he treated her like a fellow scholar of the Bard and the wonders of the stage.

She and Papa had read *Julius Caesar, King John*, and *A Midsummer Night's Dream* together while he was in hospital. They were halfway through *The Tempest* when he died. She had not the heart to pick up their Shakespeare, full of his annotations since. She thought they would finish reading all of Mr.

Shakespeare's work when he came home. Now, all she had was his well-worn book.

Sergeant Harrigan's nieces had worked their sewing machine on the rich silk damask of both their dresses. Ursula's was plumb colored and hers a blushing peach. Their weave caught the chandelier's light. Their dresses' simple pleating and off the shoulder neckline were more modest than the attire of other ladies in neighboring theater boxes, but Penina did not mind.

How they laughed together as they practiced walking and sitting in cage crinolines, their pyramid shape swung elegantly toward the back. Little Henry had gone missing amid the excitement until he emerged, crawling out from under his mother's skirts. Ursula had finally taken Penina's suggestion to forego her snood and let her beautiful hair be braided and pinned back with silk purple bellflowers and lilies of the valley. Mrs. Bell had arranged Penina's hair with her deft touch, ironed her blond curls to glistening and placed a silk orange blossom wreath over them.

"By heaven, don't you both look glorious?" Sergeant Harrigan had said as he handed them into their carriage. Penina thought she saw his hand slip around her silent mother's waist as they stood together and waved. She wished they had come. But they had decided to keep Baby Henry and his Tante company for the night. The widow of Gramercy Park did not demonstrate her hurt feelings, but the truth of it was her mother had been a better friend to Ursula before she knew the extent of her generosity.

Since the celebration of the soldiers on Rikers Island at the end of summer, Ursula all but disappeared from their lives. Henry's French Tante continued to maintain the Gramercy Park house, emptied of all but the echoes of Ursula's pianoforte and her baby's happy chortles. That lady welcomed her visits, sat her beside the kitchen fire with her maple sugar cakes and long letters from her friend. Ursula dwelled somewhere close, close enough for hand deliveries of those letters.

Ursula's letters were full of questions about their shop and her latest creations. She wrote back to her friend before the end of each visit and left the letters in the French housekeeper's care. Penina never had anyone to correspond with before, and she enjoyed it immensely.

But when Mr. Booth and his little daughter discovered her tending Ursula's garden, those sad eyes of his extracted the whole story of Ursula's mysterious disappearance and correspondence. Penina was not sorry, because she delivered the invitation from Edwin

Booth and that is what brought her to this night— Ursula was coming out of her mysterious location by popular demand, to attend the benefit performance of Mr. Shakespeare's *Julius Caesar.*

Penina tried to put her mother's coldness toward their friend from her mind now. They were about to see not one, but three members of the Booth family, portraying Brutus, Cassius and Marc Antony. And it was raising funding for the statue of Shakespeare, in the people's park, as Papa always called the grand construction of a vernal paradise in the middle of the island of Manhattan. He told her to go there often, to feel the kiss of nature within this vast city.

The scenery and costumes and costumes transported the stage back in time to the days of the ancient Roman republic. It was hard to believe that the very next night it was scheduled to be transformed again, this time into the 8th century Danish court for one hundred nights of Edwin Booth's *Hamlet.* The theater was indeed magic.

And how her father would love this theater. Penina began a letter to him in her mind. Papa, there are no less than two thousand people sitting around us. I am in a boxed seat, along with Ursula. We are flanked by her brother and husband, both quite resplendent in their dress uniforms. Behind us in the box sit members of the press, already scribbling notes and quick bird's eye views of the patrons across from and below us in the orchestra seats. Ours were reserved for us by the Booth brothers. Their mother and sisters are all wearing silk flowers in their hair of my creation, and I have painted their fans.

It is all due to your kindness towards Sergeant Kingsley and his sister, long ago. I used the comb you delivered to her while she was in convent school. I used it to sweep her pretty hair off her brow. I felt close to you then, Papa, but I so wish you were here. What did Ursula give you in return so long ago? It cannot be as valuable as this gift of her friendship.

The theater lights dimmed, the stage lights glowed. The play began.

Junius was the smallest Booth brother at five feet but projected a fierce expression that people likened to a caged tiger. Penina thought he looked more like a dragon about to breathe fire at any moment. It was most frightening as he portrayed Cassius of the 'lean and hungry look.' Older, but almost as handsome as his brothers but he was bowlegged. Was that because he was used to riding through the vast wilds of the American west?

Penina almost did not recognize the youngest acting brother, John Wilkes, as he looked every inch the noble Roman Mark Antony with his mustache shaved. And so passionate, such is his conflict between loyalty and his fight against tyranny.

Oh, but Brutus, played by Ursula's favorite Booth brother Edwin commanded the stage. He held the play together. Her papa was right about him, he was the best of them.

When the clanging of the fire department's engines sounded as the three were conspiring against Caesar, Ursula's gloved hand grasped hers. The curtain came down abruptly. Members of the audience below rose. A few of the women screamed. Their soldiers stood, each placing a protective hand on Penina and Ursula's shoulders. They all looked behind them. The newspapermen were gone.

From the side of the stage, Edwin Booth appeared and stood before the closed curtain. His presence seemed to calm the patrons before he even spoke.

"Ladies and gentlemen, please remain in your places. I have consulted with our theater manager. The firemen entered our lobby by mistake. There is a small fire in the adjacent Lafarge House Hotel. It has already been contained. We will go on with the play in a short time. Please. Return to your seats. There is no danger to us."

Ursula's hold on Penina's hand eased.

But her men remained stating.

"Lafarge," Captain Buckley said.

"Lovejoys, Metropolitan, St. James, St. Nicholas," Sergeant Kingsley recited.

"Astor House, Belmont, Fifth Avenue, Howard."

In the distance, more fire alarms sounded.

"Let's go," the captain decided.

"We cannot leave them," his brother-in-law objected.

"You're right, brother." he pulled Ursula to her feet as his sergeant was doing the same with Penina.

Jonathan Kingsley touched her nose as if she was five, before handing her her shawl. "They stab Caesar because Calpurnia was right as wives are, always. Then, from Marc Anthony, "Friends, Romans, Countrymen, lend me your ears," and all that."

"I know the speech," Penina told him.

"Good. Recite it for us in the carriage, little sister."

***

His own next speech came when they were heading down Broadway, too slowly and in the way of the firemen and their engines. "My kingdom for a horse," he said.

"The stable next to our millinery," Penina suggested, "they will have them saddled for you in no time."

When they arrived, Penina talked to the stable master while the captain kissed his wife long and hard. They were charging down the street before the screams for help started.

"Can you see anything?" Ursula called up to the coachman.

"Smoke and people coming out of Barnum's Museum, Ma'am," he answered.

"Will you join me in rendering assistance, Penina?" she asked quietly.

There was nothing quiet about her response. "Yes, please!" she said, climbing into the carriage.

Ursula hesitated a moment, as she noticed the men pulling up in a carriage behind them.

"Very good. Lead on, Mrs. Major," one of them said.

Ursula shook her head and pulled Penina inside.

"Who are they?" Penina asked.

"The fleet footed men of the press. Let us hope they can stay out of the way."

They did, watching and scribbling as Ursula went to work for the distressed people pouring out the doors of Barnum's Museum, Penina at her right hand. Their coats went to patrons who had neglected to fetch theirs before fleeing. Then their shawls covered the shoulders of shivering children. Penina did not feel cold, especially when she followed Ursula's lead and relieved two ushers who were trying to assist an extremely tall woman who was coughing and crying about not fitting through a window to make her escape.

"You are safe now," Ursula crooned reaching high to sweep a few cinders from the young woman's sleeve. The sleeve was wet, as was the bodice of her dress. Ursula asked another woman for a blanket from the stack she carried.

"If it reaches the stairwell," her distressed Scottish brogue rolled out, "Ach, if it reaches the waxworks—"

"It will not," Penina tried to assure her in that same calm voice her friend was using with the victims, "The firemen are coming."

"All of Broadway is alerted," Ursula said.

The blanket barely covered the girl's middle and sleeve but her teeth's chattering eased.

"Is that what your men are doing, Ursula?" Penina asked. "Alerting the firemen? Telling them where the fires are?"

"I believe so."

"Like Paul Revere?"

"Exactly."

"But how do they know where to send them?"

"Now that is their secret, is it not?"

"Those are lovely hats," the giant woman said, smiling shyly.

"Why, thank you," Ursula answered. "Penina makes them."

The girl coughed out her surprise. "Would you make one for me?"

"Of course. It would be our honor, Miss Swan."

She blushed. "Anna Swan, Mr. Barnum's Nova Scotia giantess I am, yes. You know me by my size."

"And your voice," Penina told her. "I have heard you sing. when I visited the museum with my mother. She said it was almost as sweet as Jenny Lind's."

Anna Swan turned to Ursula. "Why, thank you, that was most kind, Madame," she said.

Before Penina could correct her notion that Ursula was her mother, they were joined by a giant man in full French Army uniform and gold braid epaulettes, carrying a baby. No, not a baby, Penina realized, it was General Grant Junior, a very small man. And the giant man was—

"Monsieur Josef!" Anna cried out. "You and our petit general are safe?"

"Mais bien sûr!"

"We have lost only our hats," said the little man.

"Oh, do not worry, gentlemen," Miss Swan assured them. "These ladies can make you new ones."

Chapter Twenty Four ~ Magnus

November 26, 1864

The men seemed more involved in enjoying their sausages and reading of their exploits than explaining their abject failure to fulfill the mission. A grumbling Phil loaded their plates again.

"Why did you not open a window of your hotel rooms?" she demanded.

"It was cold, Ma'am."

"Cold? Cold?" Magnus demanded. "Of course it was cold, this is the end of November."

"In New York, not Kentucky," Jacob Thompson reminded him.

"That's what ignites Greek Fire. Air! How many times did I tell you that?"

Bob Kenner shrugged. "I do not think it would have made a difference. There was not much of a breeze."

"I am disgusted with the lot of you. All you have done is strengthened this godless city's resolve. And ignited a manhunt. Wait for the last train across the river." Magnus reached into his vest's inside pocket. "Here are your tickets. Travel separately. Meet in Montreal. And keep your smiles wide, but mouths shut, they are questioning all Southerners."

"But no one will bother with ancient Mr. and Mrs. Charles," Phil reminded him. "We should remain. Merely an auntie and uncle, enjoying the sights."

Magnus nodded. "I agree." With the manhunt on, he and Phil could formulate another plan. There were vials of Greek Fire left. They would not need a competent crew to further this plan. They had a propellant waiting. At the Gas Works.

Jack Headley was still lost in his reading. "Anna. She did not fit through the window. And her sleeve caught on fire. She was so frightened."

"Anna who?"

"Anna Swan. The Nova Scotia giantess."

"Killed?"

"No. The mermaid doused her with her tank water. But, my Anna. It says that she screamed, inhaling smoke, that awful blue smoke we made. We had a conversation, when I visited the museum. She sang a few verses of *The Bonnie Banks o' Loch Lomond* for me. Has it ruined her voice, I wonder? Why did you go to the Barnum Museum, Bob?"

Kenner shrugged. "I was finished with my hotels. I had three tubes left over."

"It says here that Barnum's lecture hall was full. There was a terrible panic."

"That was the idea, Jack. Striking fear, causing panic."

"Poor Anna."

"There is a charming drawing in the Herald," Jacob Thompson pointed out, "of two of the theatergoers offering assistance. How tiny they look next to Anna. How beautiful they are. They must be sisters."

Magnus Kingsley's eyes scanned the illustration, then grabbed it away, putting it before Phil.

"Look. She is showing herself."

"Who, sir?" Thompson asked.

Magnus ignored the question.

Ursula

Ursula kissed her husband's singed eyebrows when she woke from her nightmare of losing him to the war that had come to this city. He slept on. What would it be like to awake every morning beside him? She dared not think about it for more than a moment each morning they had together. But she wondered if her heart would burst with happiness.

Well, best not to wake her exhausted men and sleepy baby with her early morning habits. They were ensconced in a full house where every bed was providing rest for her overnight guests—Miriam and Mr. Bell, Dibb and Nima were in the third-floor rooms, as Marie Agathe had taken up residence in the housekeeper's quarters below stairs. Rowan and Jonathan set up a camp bed for Penina in the space of her choosing, the library. The house seemed to breathe with exhausted, well-earned sleep.

But the crisp morning air was calling her.

Ursula loved the Gramercy gardens in all seasons. Even now, as all her flowers and medicinals were put to bed for the upcoming winter, it held the promise of life. As her city did, after the danger that had visited her the night before.

What a triumph the Booth brothers' performance of *Julius Caesar* at the Winter Garden had been. But the bigger triumph was made by of the two men she loved best in the world. Theirs would likely remain secret, or others would take credit. But the streets of New York would remember, would honor the night they helped keep her adopted city from a fiery destruction. Why? To become a better place. Perhaps to become what the New World was for Rowan, and fellow starving peoples all over the world. A refuge. Not for scoundrels, murderers and slave stealers, but for people like him.

The figure wrapped in a woolen shawl and slumped on the iron bench had an early edition of The Times rolled and fisted tightly in one hand. Was he practicing his opening scene of Hamlet? He looked the very image of the Melancholy Dane. Perhaps she should not disturb him. But he was so lightly dressed, and she knew how susceptible he was to infections of his throat, and what they did to his beautiful voice. She approached, wanting to send him inside by his own fire's warmth.

His hand grasped hers. "Mrs. Major. I was hoping you'd resumed your early morning walks. Our wise, gentle Ursula, I need your good counsel. For I fear I have splintered my family forever."

"Edwin, it is too cold for you to be without your coat."

"That is of no consequence," he growled out. "Walk with me?"

"Of course. That will warm us both." His grip on the newspaper tightened fiercely. "Last night was a great triumph," she prompted. "Did the critics not agree?"

"We urged Wilkes to read reviews that singled out his fine performance, the fullness of his elocution. I spoke about another benefit for us in late April, after my hundred days of *Hamlet*. Of *Romeo and Juliet*, with him playing Romeo, climbing trellises with those well-formed calves the ladies swoon over. But he would have none of it. He would read only of the fires of last night. And that lit our own conflagration. Oh, Ursula. I threw our brother out."

"What happened?"

"You know we have banned all talk of our differing politics for our mother's sake?"

"Yes, I remember your pledge."

"But this morning…if you could have heard him, Ursula. I think he is ill again, and it has afflicted his mind. We have hardly seen him since nursing him back to health this summer. Off he went to his oil fields of Pennsylvania. We urged him to get back on stage, but he brushed us aside. After reading us the news of last evening, he would not join in our dismay—dismay over a city in flames, of lives lost if the plan had succeeded.

"Our brother June opined that in San Francisco the arsonists would have been rounded up by the city's vigilantes and hanged forthwith. But I think it was what I said that sparked the fuse."

"What did you say?"

"I broke our mother's commandment, Ursula. I said I blamed our city's distress on the war. And that I hoped my first vote—a vote for Lincoln—would help us to achieve peace at last."

"Your vote. Politics."

"Exactly. Wilke's anger exploded. He said the fires were retaliation for the destruction that the Union Army brought as it marched through the Shenandoah Valley and Georgia. He said I would regret my vote when Lincoln was crowned king. And that he would ever be a true Southerner. That he still hoped for the success of the Rebellion."

Ursula winced. "And your response?"

"You have intuited it, as always, dear lady. I told him he should go elsewhere to make such sentiments known. That he was not at liberty to express them in the house of a Union supporter."

"There now. There is a road back."

"I fear not. And, worse. Oh, Ursula, I fear I shall never see my brother again. My friend. All my life has been on picket duty, it seems, on guard for disasters. When they come, I am prepared. To others, I seem callous in my response. Only you know my anguish. 'There is a special providence in the fall of a sparrow,'" he began. And waited.

"'If it be now, tis not to come;'" she whispered.

He nodded. "'If it be not to come, it will be now;'" he said.

"'If it be not now, yet it will come.'"

"'The readiness is all,'" he finished, heading back to his home.

He was out of her sight when Ursula heard Marie Agathe's scream.

Magnus

New York Gas Light Company's 21 Street Works ran from coal furnaces. Their belching smokestacks were only three blocks from the bucolic confines of Gramercy Park. At his knocked signal, Phil opened the great iron door of the boiler room.

"You have the brat?" she asked.

"Well, I have a brat." Magnus yanked his captive from the carriage and pulled the hood off an unconscious Penina.

"Where's her baby?"

"This one shoved the baby and the housekeeper into the stairwell and that damned woman locked the door and started waking the whole household. I would be outnumbered in moments. It is lucky your ether acts fast, or I would not have gotten hold of this one."

"She is no one. We need the baby!"

"I think not. My dear step-daughter is attached to this girl. I hope I have not killed her."

"It matters little. You did leave the ransom note?"

"Shoved it under the door."

"Bring her along. The stokers are tucked in nicely at the end of their workday, poor lambs," she said in her Auntie voice. "Victims of my gift of breakfast biscuits." Her tone shifted to Mother Superior. "I have placed the vials by the gasometers near the main governor that distributes the gas along. Soon the foremen will abandon their posts to investigate the dwindling fires, giving us passage. We have half an hour to finish this."

"Good work, Mrs. Charles."

Chapter Twenty Five ~ Ursula

Caroline and Sergeant Harrigan stood waiting beyond the garden gate. "Good God," Ursula whispered as she grabbed the hands of her husband and brother. "They have come to escort Penina home."

"Leave them to me," Jonathan assured them. "Go, go. I will catch up to you."

Whatever he said made them move towards her house. Good, Ursula thought. Caroline and her policeman were more guardians for the baby.

When they reached the imposing brick building, she eased out of the carriage first.

"I must go in alone, my darlings," she said. "It is what the note requires."

"No."

"Do not move until I am inside. If our Penina comes to harm, I shall never forgive myself. Please."

They bowed their heads and released her.

***

Inside, the woman she once knew as Sister Philomena took a cruel grip of her arm. Ursula felt the tip of a knife at her back.

"Without a word," the woman hissed. "Like in our old days together, novice. I have skills, thanks to your friends placing me into the kitchen of that hospital in Washington. Butchering skills."

This was a hellish inverse of their convent days and their imposed silences, Ursula thought as they traveled through labyrinthine passageways and open metal stairways. Instead of the smell of incense and the hum of prayer at lauds and vespers, the coal baking furnaces thrummed and gave off noxious fumes.

How would her beloveds ever find her?

They passed a black-suited man slumped over beside his telegraph key.

"Resourceful lad. But any help he might have summoned will come too late."

She was not coming to bargain for Penina's release, Ursula realized. They intended to kill them both.

The imposing form of her step-father filled a doorway. "Welcome to hell, my darling daughter. As promised, your sleepy little admirer, delivered." He stepped over the still form of Penina at his feet. "Mrs. Charles, kindly keep watch for her brave soldiers."

It was his charming voice. The one he used to coax her mother out of her grief. Warm, welcoming, modest. Ready for a game of whist, a walk along the shore collecting shells.

"It is a little sad, I think," that voice continued, "that once they have sorted through the flames, you will be getting more credit than you deserve. You will live on in infamy while we only get to survive in a world cleansed of devil abolitionists, defying God's order. It hardly seems fair. We shall have to live well, in your honor."

He came closer. She could smell him—and his rotten tooth, treated with whiskey, but badly infected. A swollen left cheek. Still, he smiled. "My, my. At last, a good look at you. No longer a child. A fulsome woman, my former little Bride of Christ." He laughed and the tone changed, became laced with rage. "Whore of Christ. Damned nuns, keeping you from me all those years. Until Phil pulled the ladder out from under your precious Rafaela. She was in a hurry to take the reins over you."

Not an accident, then. Oh, dear woman, forgive me, Ursula prayed. Sister Rafaela's admonition rang at her ears. "Ursula. You are the sinned against, not the sinning."

"How does it feel to sacrifice yourself to the cause?" he asked.

No more silences. Ursula lifted her chin. "Lost cause."

"There has always been slavery!"

"And there has always been resistance."

He slapped her hard enough to create a ringing in her ears. She heard her hairpins pinging on the floor of the gasworks, as they had in the root cellar, long ago.

"This day the war turns back in our direction, enslaving your Miriam again, and her precious Sling, and those sour-faced daughters, who bleated like lambs when I—Ah, but you wanted me, not my dull-eyed cousin as your bridegroom, did you not, seductress? That is why you refused his suit. You wanted my righteous anger, you wanted me to do what I did. Say it!"

"You blighted my mother's family, and Miriam's. We were the sinned against, not the sinning."

"You were born in sin, temptress. Did you tell your Irishman about me, Ursula? No? Is he here, listening, now?"

Philomena's eyes skirted along the way they had come. "What is wrong with you? Kill her. Let us be done and set this city ablaze."

"Always in a rush, Phil. That is what tripped you up once that Irishman went from patient to her besotted champion, that's what got your kinsman killed."

"Your son chose her over you, too," she reminded him with a cruel smile.

"That whelp is none of mine."

Captain Kane appeared beside an iron girder. "I shall be happy to claim him."

Jonathan. On the side of another girder. "Why, thank you, sir. I accept."

And finally, Rowan stepped out.

They were too close, Ursula thought. But her beloveds were safe, for once. Because Magnus Kingsley lunged, not for them, but for her.

She aimed her fist for that rotted tooth. It hit its mark. He howled, staggered back. Then Penina sprang and brought him down.

***

Ursula heard the clanging of fire wagons, was swept past Mr. Bell, calmly removing vials of Greek fire into the hands of his statuesque assistants Dibb and Nima, who placed each into his padded carpet bag. Nima, waiting for the next, looked up, smiled and nodded. To her, to the man who held her. Rowan. Yes, his infantry frock coat's shoulder straps attached with shoestring ties passing through Marie Agathe's sturdy, hand-whipped eyelets.

Then they were outside in the cold November air and his coat was about her shoulders and she was set on her feet again.

"Breathe, 'Sula," Rowan said in his captain voice.

No more secrets. She looked down at her raw knuckled hand. "I gave birth to a child, Rowan. A child by that man."

"Shhh," he said, holding her close, his lips pressing at her temple.

"How can you bear to touch me?" she whispered.

His arms tightened. She could not move. She could see only one of his eyes, the beautiful blue glass one. It was the only false thing about him. She had to see the other.

But he lifted his head, searching the early morning sky. For what? The constellation he'd once sworn to always find her by? She was no longer his Ursa Major, mother bear to his beautiful son. Did he wonder how the stars had betrayed him, too?

His arms did not release her, but they shook. His whole body shook. She felt her face, her neck, wet. Not with her own tears this time. Her brave, strong husband was weeping as he struggled to find his voice amid the whirlwind.

"Ursula, hear me," it finally proclaimed as if he was reciting one of the Irish sagas he already told their son at bedtime, "You are made of stars."

***

Caroline sent Penina out for a walk in Gramercy Park, accompanied by Sergeant Harrigan, who had been very good at managing great numbers of police and firemen who found twelve more hidden vials of Greek Fire hidden among straw bales propped up against the walls of the New York Gas Light Company.

Sunlight streamed though the lace curtains, illuminating her books and Henry's wooden pull duck. Marie Agathe set out the tea and slices of her maple sugar cake and left the library. Ursula poured, thinking that the moments ahead would mark the end of her friendship with Caroline Selby. She held Rowan's handkerchief tightly in her lap. She longed for him, for her brother, for her baby. But she must bear this loss alone.

Caroline spoke softly. "Forgive me for not telling you what I am about to sooner. I had to know you very well, and move past our misunderstandings, before I made this choice. I had to know you did not mean harm."

"Harm?"

"To Penina and me."

"How could I ever think to harm you?"

"Ursula, my husband was of a people that have been accused of terrible things: kidnappings, murders of children, blood libel. This is done through ignorance, and prejudices in Christian communities. Even among my own."

"But we thought the world of your husband, Jonathan and I, from back in the days of our childhood."

"And I hope, after, you will continue to hold us in… in some esteem."

"After what?" Tears falling down Caroline Selby's face, threatening Ursula's own sympathetic ones. Oh, this would not do. But how could dear Mr. Shulmann's wife think so ill of her?

"Mrs. Major," Caroline finally said, "I am fifty-four years old."

Ursula would have guessed many years younger, between the woman's health and vigor. Her face had only the kind of creases that laughter brings around her eyes. But this was not the time for compliments, so she remained silent, listening. Wondering why she was the formal "Mrs. Major" again.

Caroline Selby drank a swallow of tea and replaced it to its saucer. "When I had reached the age of forty, I was experiencing my fifth childbearing. I had lost all our babies before their sixth month inside me. When I quickened with this fifth, Mr. Shulmann took funds meant for the purchase of our own shop to rent a pretty little house in the country outside Baltimore, instead of our city boarding house. My Aaron continued to travel his peddling route from the Eastern Shore plantations across Maryland's border with Pennsylvania and Virginia, leaving me now within our cottage, with people hired to help with the cooking, washing, cleaning. So that I could be off my feet and thriving, along with the little one growing inside me, you see? Those months were a happy time. Over his Sunday visits we grew foolish and thought we would become Mama and Papa at last."

This was the story of Penina's birth, born after all that grieving, Ursula thought.

"But our son was a seventh month child. He came too quickly even to send for the midwife. Born into his father's hands. Still born."

"Oh. Oh, no."

"I could not give him up. Not for hours. The dear little face. My Aaron made a beautiful pine box for him, like the others. I knew in my heart that he was our last chance. My courses were already changing— lightening, growing further apart.

"I convinced Aaron to resume his work, his travels. Still, I could not give the dream of that baby up. Even my body would not accept our loss. 'A shame, enough milk for twins,' the midwife said, as she gave me cloths for binding my breasts, and left me with tinctures. I did not take them, or bind. I wanted my baby. And if I could not have him, I wanted to die. My breasts became hard, painful, I became fevered. My husband found me this way at the end of the week and saved me."

The woman went suddenly silent, staring down at her hands.

"How?" Ursula breathed out.

Caroline raised her head. "By putting a baby to my breast. A tiny baby who came too soon, like my own, but breathing. I will never forget my husband's eyes, bright with hope. "'Ask your wife to care for her, just until she dies,' they bid me, Caroline. But we will not allow her to die, will we, my love?" he said, as he tucked her into bed beside me. Her suckling was weak, and I was so engorged she could barely latch on. But at the sound of her cry the milk flowed, drop by drop into her mouth. The first milk, still yellow. She was perfect, only so small, with soft hairs on her back and ears and half-grown nails on her fingers and toes.

"From that first day I knew she would survive, and so would I. So we gave her what the nuns did not: a name."

Nuns. Ursula felt her own milk descend and stain her bodice. "What does it mean, her name?" she asked, frightened by the flat tone of her own voice.

"Pearl. Penina means pearl, because she is our hidden treasure."

"And... mine?"

"Yes, my dear Ursula. And yours."

Ursula was transported back. To the tiny hand, blue and lifeless, its nails half-grown. To her pleas to see her daughter's face before they swept her away. Pearl. Mr. Shulmann told Jonathan that she had given them a pearl. She had, without knowing it. Until now.

The secrets swirled there, about her skirts. Did Sister Raphaela know? Of course she did. She had contacted Mr. Gardner, who hid the Shulmann family in the bustling streets of New York.

Ursula now understood her lawyer's shock when their lives connected to the Selbys through a girl's hunger to return to her garden.

The past loss, the dangerous present. Retreat. Retreat into silence. Ursula battled with her body's command to shut down, escape it all.

No. Go back. Remember. If she could not raise her head, at least raise her voice.

"Sister Raphaela baptized her. My baby had taken three breaths, enough to enter the kingdom of heaven, she said."

Was that her voice? It must have been, for Caroline Selby reached across the space between them in response, to squeeze her hands.

But Caroline's voice was like frightened birds. "When I married my Aaron, we were both shunned. We observed a family philosophy that observed customs of both our former faiths. But we raised Penina to love and honor all. You remember him well, my Aaron, on his visits to your family at Fenwick Pines, do you not?"

This was real, this woman's fear. Of her. "Yes," Ursula whispered.

"He did not steal your child!"

Say something. "Of course not, no."

"Ursula, your baby. She saved my life."

Ursula looked up from the floorboards, from her own skirts. Find it. Find the breath to ease this woman's suffering. "As you saved hers. When did you know?"

"I fought all the signs—the striking resemblance among the three of you—Penina and you and Sergeant Kingsley. The way you sparred and doted on him marked you as brother and sister even before Penina told me it was so. So you were both connected to my Aaron when he was a peddler. Still, I did not think it possible that you gave birth to Penina. You are so young. Then Sergeant Kingsley confided to me that Captain Buckley is your husband and that they stole you out of a convent. I know why some girls are sent into convents."

"It was not Penina's fault, how she came to be."

"Neither was it yours. You are not yet thirty. You were a child."

"Yes. Caught by an enraged man, when I refused his bidding. Caroline, our Penina, our beautiful girl, she is the child of rape."

"Oh. Oh, my dear. Does your brother— "

"By his father. My mother's husband."

"Merciful God."

"Perhaps. But that man showed me none."

"The one who sought your inheritance. Which is so large he was willing to share it with your church. All is falling into place. Ursula, did your brother know? Did your husband?"

"Not until this morning. When he took Penina…Caroline, there was so much suffering. I wanted no more suffering on my hands."

"My dear, none of this was by your hand."

"But you do not know— "

"I know you. And who you were, a high-spirited girl, like my Penina, before evil came into your life. You were not safe this morning. Neither were our children."

"Must we tell Penina?" Ursula asked her wiser friend.

"Yes, my love, I think we must."

She twisted the handkerchief she had used to dry her husband's tears. "How will she— ?"

"That, we will learn together."

Penina

It was like their first meeting in the kitchen of her townhouse, with her men in their rolled-up shirt-sleeves, and good things cooking on the hearth, and in the warming oven. Even Baby Henry was there, on Captain Buckley's lap, playing with the miraculous medal he had pulled by its chain from inside his father's shirt.

But Penina had banished her mother to the library.

She took the yoke back chair that Sergeant Kingsley set out, across from Ursula. A burst of anger flared from her like a flame.

"You are not my mother!"

A flinch. And those wounded eyes. Not what she meant to do, no.

Then came that calm, modulated voice, sounding like when Ursula's fingers traveled over the piano keys. "I gave birth to you. Your mother gave you life." She bit her lip. "Do you need her now, Penina? At this moment?"

"No. I do not want to hurt her. But I want, I want…

"

"To be yourself, freely?" Sergeant Kingsley asked.

"Yes, that."

Ursula's fingers twitched, there in her lap. They had been friends, once.

Penina found her voice again. "You left me."

"No. The sisters told me you died."

"All of them? Even your precious Rafaela?"

"Yes."

"Why?"

"They thought it best."

"It was not their choice to make."

"No. It was not."

"You did not leave me?" Penina demanded now.

"No."

"Or give me away?"

"No."

"Or try to be rid of me? Or wish me to die?"

"I have missed you every day."

"Are you angry with Mr. Gardner and the nuns? For keeping me a secret?"

"A little," Ursula admitted.

"And, my parents? Are you angry with them?"

"No. Yours is a beautiful story."

"Papa was a Jew. I do not know what I am. But I am no Catholic!"

"This matters not at all to me."

"You do not hate me because I am from … that man who hurt you?"

Jonathan stepped out of the shadow of the hearth. "No more than she hates me, niece."

"Sergeant Kingsley." Penina blinked twice. "I am your sister."

"Yes. That, too."

"Our father—"

Jonathan crossed his arms and leaned back against the stone wall. "He gave up his right to that honor long ago. Ursula once gave me her own father to replace him. You may have her husband as yours."

Penina raised her eyes to Rowan's. "Captain Buckley?"

He smiled. "If you will have me, lass."

"I have two mothers," she told him.

"I had four."

"Your own, and the three Maries?"

"Just so. A person can never have too many mothers. The Maries remind me of that often."

"Captain. Henry is my brother? My baby brother?"

"If you will have him."

The baby in question slipped off his lap and toddled into her arms.

Rowan's smile widened. "He seems as eager as I that you do."

Epilogue

Belle Haven, Ashoken-on-Hudson, New York

July 16, 1865

Rowan

As he looked across at Ursula, with Henry in her lap and Penina beside her, Rowan felt his heart breaking. By the end of this day, he would know if he was losing yet another family. He did not know if he could survive this parting.

But first, duty. His first superior, Captain Merritt had sent them here, upriver from Ursula's house, on an errand of mercy. To visit his Columbia University schoolmate, Captain Cole, who had treated Rowan's injuries after Antietam, who had chosen and fitted him with his glass eye. The war had not gone well for the physician after their parting. He had barely survived his confinement in Libby Prison. Exchanged, he'd been sent home to die. But Captain Merritt said Ryder

273

Cole's indomitable mother had other plans. So, Rowan was to present himself as another war casualty, also once left for dead. As the holy possibility for another man, whose mother had plans for him.

And Rowan knew better than to get in the way of a strong woman's plans. He was part of Ursula's rehabilitation of her friend Edwin Booth, was he not? After his brother brought President Lincoln down at war's end, they worked together to testify that Edwin was ever loyal to the Union cause. Plunged into grief for both country and family, the actor remained determined to keep with his vow never to appear on stage again. But he was beginning to favor them with Shakespearian readings in Ursula's parlor. Could his return as Hamlet in his beloved Winter Garden theater be far behind?

And now, a visit to this man they both knew, the doctor who had urged Rowan to profess his love to a woman who had dedicated herself as a Bride of Christ.

Both the grand house that was built when the country was new, and its hostess were welcoming to their visitors. The receiving room looked like the courtyard of ancient Roman villas Rowan had seen in the history books of Ursula's library. Mrs. Cole had the same dark, intense-eyed beauty as Rowan remembered about her son. But Captain Cole himself, propped up in his finely carved four poster bed, was a shadow of the man Rowan remembered. He'd suffered a massive apoplexy while a prisoner and its impairments were evident. But those leaf-green eyes lit with recognition, and somehow, Rowan felt an immediate, deep connection that his own Irish mother would have called "beyond the veil."

He brought Ursula forward. "You know us both, do you not, sir?" Rowan asked.

Captain Cole's mouth slowly formed itself around a word. "Eye?"

Rowan nodded. "Yes, sir. My glass eye is holding up something fine. A good choice. And as you can see, I took your advice, to tell Sister Ursula that I loved her beyond the beyond. And would you look at the reward for my courage in doing so? May I present these two beauties of creation that came with her: lovely Penina and that little scalawag looking to climb your bedpost is our Henry."

Penina held out her bouquet of flowers with a curtsy, drawing Henry from his mother's arms to scamper after them.

"Closer?" Captain Cole implored.

Henry crawled up past the yellow roses to Captain Cole, resting his chubby elbows on the man's chest, causing Captain Cole's sharp intake of breath.

"Is he hurting you, darling?" his mother asked.

"No, no. So beautiful."

Mrs. Cole cast her shining eyes on her guests. "Two! Two sentences!" she proclaimed.

Rowan sat beside his doctor on his bed and reached out his arms for his son. "You'd best get well before your own need chasing, Captain."

Dr. Cole looked away. "Lost," he breathed out.

Who did he mean? All the soldiers he cared for now dead of violence or disease? Rowan put his hand on the man's shoulder and got his answer as he remembered the young sergeant, who the doctor loved and called Tom. Rowan knew Tom was not a man but promised to keep her secret. Mrs. Cole said the war had claimed their sergeant. But Rowan felt her living presence there, in this moment, in his bones. He closed his eyes and saw her even more clearly. She was not alone. She was beneath a tree, giving birth to their tiny daughter.

"Keep on with your healing, Captain," he found himself saying. "You will find them."

***

"Why did you tell him that?" Ursula asked as they walked the house's winding path grounds after taking refreshments with Mrs. Cole in her drawing room.

"I cannot say, 'Sula."

"Why?"

"Because I do not know, lass."

"It was your heart speaking? As when you found me as the motherhouse burned, led by your sister? Your sister, who died so long ago?"

"Yes."

"Your pronouncement today produced a wonderful effect. I believe Captain Cole's mother would like to adopt us all now."

"Well. We can never have too many mothers, can we?" He took her hand. "Listen. I need to take you to a place Mrs. Cole told me of, down the road, perched on some rocks, overlooking the Hudson."

She nodded. "Henry is asleep in the library while Penina is devouring Mrs. Cole's books on horticulture. And I would like you alone for part of today." She smiled. "My long-delayed birthday gift to myself. Wait here. I will tell them our plans and fetch my lovely shawl, shall I?"

His gift. To honor her birthday. Her thirtieth birthday, which came at the end of the war, days after the sorrow filled end of their president. Today would come the reckoning. He had to be a man, and accept her decision. But it took all the courage he had to say, "aye, then."

Ursula

Rowan brought her to a simple pedimented, four columned structure that looked like a Greek temple kissed by the sun at this golden hour, when its rays slanted down on the water. But her husband, his eyes the same deep blue as his dress uniform, was dragging his feet like a schoolboy who wanted a day at the fishing hole instead.

The structure was a chapel built a generation before. It was the first Catholic church north of Manhattan, meant to serve the foundry families of the small town, many of them new arrivals from Ireland. Perhaps Rowan's family would have come here, had they survived Grosse Isle. They sat on the stone steps together, watching a sloop catch the upriver current.

"That looks heavenly and quiet, unlike the clacking train or rumbling steamships. We could sail almost to your part of Canada, could we not?"

"Aye."

What was the source of his melancholy? It was not like him, but Ursula had sensed it since the spring that brought the end of the war coupled with the murder of a president. "Do you miss your own country, Rowan? Your farm and the Maries?"

"I do." Fear gripped her heart. He frowned as he looked across the river, at the Army fortress of West Point. "'Sula. Mr. Gardner explained it to me. What this last birthday of yours means."

She did not like the direction this conversation was going. Not at all. A nervous, skittering laugh sprang from her as she pulled her shawl closer.

"It means I have your lovely gift to keep off the evening breeze's chill. Thank you, Rowan."

"Penina chose the pattern."

"But not the color. She offered up the crimson, and you told her I favor the blues."

He smiled ruefully. "I should have known you two would examine every detail of our shopping expedition."

There, better. Much better, Ursula thought. Until he took her hand.

"Mr. Gardner's paperwork is finally accomplished. This is the time we spoke of before we took our vows. I wanted us here, a sacred spot, to have it out."

"Out?" she took up his infernal Irish questioning.

But he did not ask her another one. "Aye. It is time. We said we would decide the strength of our own union after the war, after the suspicions they had against you were proven false, after you came fully into your inheritance. I do not have the wit to understand the details, but Mr. Gardner said being married to me safeguarded your estate, provided protection. Your father's will says it is all yours now that you have reached your thirtieth year."

Her dry mouth could barely form the word. "And...?" she whispered.

"And Jonathan has already mustered out of the Army, and loves New York, so you will have him close by, schooled by Mr. Gardner in your business affairs. My Army superiors, they have offered me a commission. To work out in the West, protecting the rail lines, the new settlements growing up around them, from the Indians."

"'Work?' Do you mean they have offered you a command?"

"Well, yes."

"And, do you wish to remain in the Army, Rowan?"

"No. But the time of me being of use to you? It is over."

"What of Henry? And Penina?"

"I will always be their father. I will always love them, need to look after them. I know that will make your life going forward more complicated."

"Complicated?"

"Aye. But I told Mr. Gardner I will never stand in your way."

"My way? My way?" Was that her voice, that screech? "My way where?"

"Why, wherever your will decrees. 'Sula, we both know that we are opposites. I am a poor farmer turned broken down soldier. Our paths would never have crossed but for the war, and your healing gifts. You are an accomplished person. And a woman of means. We married to protect you, and your inheritance. Except for our children, our life going forward—"

"Stop. Stop it!" Ursula stood, ran, but there was no escaping, except onto the rocks below them. She pulled in a strangled breath, and turned to face him, widening her stance. "You said I was made of stars, even after you learned that Penina is part of my inheritance. Rowan, can you not love me?"

He cocked his head as if she'd spoken a language he did not understand. "I love you more than life itself Ursula Major, do you not know that?"

"I do not! Not when you talk of fighting Indians, who never did you any harm!"

His good eye clouded with tears. "True enough. They never did. But 'Sula, did you not wish what Mr. Gardner said, to talk with me about our future?"

"No! I mean, not this."

The river breeze wafted through his black curls. The dying sun burnished the chapel behind him even more golden. But she barely took note of either, as her rage mounted. "How dare you even speak of such a thing as leaving me, Rowan Buckley? With all the good work we need to do? And with us living near rail lines into Canada, so we can spend summers with the Maries at Lacolle. We will all look after the women who raised you to a man. A whole man, of grace and beauty, never a broken one. The two sisters who ran my households in Maryland and New York, and the one I have yet to meet, your three Maries, they know you better than you know yourself, husband. Every summer we will visit them, do you hear me? We will all learn how to dance to your wild tunes and speak French and bake a decent tourtière. Do not you even think of leaving us for the west!"

An astonished smile took over his face. "The fleeting thought has perished, Mrs. Buckley," he said quietly.

"Well, that is settled."

His face looked suddenly very young, and she saw the carefree boy he once was, before all the tragedy entered his life. Then his Irish craftiness returned with a quirk of his brow.

"And what of the subject of your own making, wife? The one I mistook for your desire to be free of me?"

Ursula felt the heat rising to her cheeks, which only brought him closer. She looked down at the swirling patterns of her beautiful shawl. "I was hoping to discuss…Rowan, I am not getting any younger. And Henry is now two. So, if you thought, it might be time to work on…"

"Come now, you were not so shy about ordering my life's course a moment ago, woman. Work on what?"

She finally met his even stare. "Giving Henry and Penina a brother or sister."

His right brow disappeared into those breeze-swept curls. "So. You find me useful still."

"I do!"

"Ah, then. I finally get an enthusiastic 'I do' out of you." He took her up into his arms and kissed her breathless. "Are we well and proper married now, do you think?"

"Before God and this glorious sunset, you baneful man, we are," she assured him.

The End

If you enjoyed
this book,
please leave
the
author a
review.

Author's Note

I am deeply indebted to scholars of this period in American history, especially new and overlooked viewpoints. Special thanks to scholar Jermaine Fowler and the gifts he brings to his podcast *The Humanity Archive*. I am looking forward to many more journeys with you, Jermaine. Thank you for influencing my stories and touching my life.

Big thanks to my delightful grandson Desmond, the model for Henry Ryan Buckley, and to his mother

Marya for making sure we could hug and play with him despite miles and pandemic barriers.

Many fellow storytellers, writers, readers, friends, advocates and fine editors had a hand in my writing life over the years. I am profoundly grateful. Among them are Judith Pittman, Janet Lane Waters, Deborah Barnhart, Juilene Osborne-McKnight, Yolanda Sly, Eileen O'Finlan, Jane Willan, Liz Matis, Sunny Hogg, Ed Renahan, Claire Ruane, Mary Bloxsom, Robert Crooke, Jenna Kernan, Gianna Simonne, Kathy Attalla, Nina Shengold, Juilene Osborne-McKnight, Mark Schoen, Liz Armstrong, Natalia Aponte, Victoria Lea, Susan Wallach, Charlie Rineheimer, Mitzi Flyte, Nancy Bell, Andrea Peterson, Jane Seiver, Tim Bentler-Jungr, Jennifer Probst, Susan King, Janet Evanovich, Cindy Skaggs, Mariah Stewart, Chér Coen, Abigail Gullo, Judy Fitzwater, Nicole Quinn, Cathy Maxwell, Sarah Johnson, Minette Gunther, Andrea Sadler, Yvonne Pinney, Rosemary Morris, Bill Lockwood, Kathleen Gilles Seidel, Jonathan Kruk, Stephanie Cowell, Kathryn Anderson, Denise McInerney, Cindi Myers, Robyn Amos Pope, Laurie Treacy, Dennis Yerry, Anita Gordon, K.I. Going, Evan Pritchard, Joe Bruchac, Joanna Withey, Mary Lenaburg, Maureen Morrison, Jo-Ann Power, Pamela Manché

Pearce, Dee Oiler, Wanda Shapiro, Pam Palmer, Eileen Nauman, Lawrence Gullo and Fyodor Pavlov.

I have a special love and appreciation for local booksellers and libraries and all they do for authors, readers and their communities. We have great ones in Célina and crew at the Rockingham Public Library and Pat, Alan and Myles at Village Square Booksellers here in Bellows Falls, Vermont.

Eileen Charbonneau's stories explore the perspectives of people often left out of history: women, first peoples and immigrants, marginalized poor.

Eileen has published fiction for adult as well for young readers. She lives in the brave little state of Vermont with her husband Ed. She adores him, her kids and sweet grandchild. Eileen loves reading, watching great movies, exploring her beautiful state, country and world, roots music and dance of all cultures, and Vermont maple creemies. (write to her at eileencharbonneau@gmail.com and she'll tell you what they are!)

Eileen loves to hear from readers. You can find her at:
https://bookswelove.net/charbonneau-eileen/
eileencharbonneau.com
email: eileencharbonneau@gmail.com
twitter: @EileenC1988
Facebook: Eileen Charbonneau Author
Instagram: eileencharbonneau

Blogs: http://manituwak.blogspot.com
https://bwlauthors.blogspot.com